I

CW01509182

SARAH

Before the very first day I met him, I was sitting in my office
Contract on my laptop. Although I was barely 25, I was alrea
Hutchinson & Co Legal.

It was a tiring day, a humid day, and the window at the side opened to the busy traffic at Lincoln
Heights. I stared at the second hand of the wall clock as the time edged away to 5:15pm.

A knock came on the door of my office. It was Michelle. She had a bright smile. She usually had a bright
smile around me.

Michelle walked in confidently. Her black bag looped down from her shoulder and dangled back and
forth. Michelle wore a red dress, which was smooth and wrapped neatly around her body, exposing her
alluring features and beauty. Her blonde hair cascaded down to the nape of her neck, and she constantly
pushed up the small tendrils of hair on her brow.

I kept looking up at her as she drifted down to my desk. Her height was perfect, scaling towards six feet.
I was quite tall for a woman, but Michelle was thoroughly blessed with the height of her father.

"Are you still looking through that stuff?" Michelle asked, slouching against the desk.

"I want to make sure everything is perfect."

"It is already perfect Sarah. Come on. I want you to accompany me."

"Where?"

"Shopping!"

"Another party?"

"You bet. This one is really cool. Frank Steward is celebrating his birthday."

"Who is Frank Steward? Am I was supposed to know him?"

Michelle placed a forefinger on her cheek and tapped away thoughtfully. Her bright smile featured the
genuine, smooth trajectory of her thoughts.

"You are supposed to know him. He is prominent in real estates and close friends with my father."

"Will your father be there?"

"Does it matter?"

"Maybe. You know how your parties…"

"Don't start Sarah. I know where you're headed."

"Where will that be?"

Michelle shook her head, pulled away from the table, and walked towards the window.

"You always take the humble route. I understand my privilege, Sarah. I know you're not so privileged, but do you really have to be humble and meek?"

Michelle was looking away from me. I had a feeling she didn't want to be restrained by the expression on my face.

"I am not sure I really understand you," I said, standing up from my chair.

"You understand Sarah. You're about to question whether you deserve to be at the party because you know I'm going to invite you."

"No...I was just curious... You know... I just want to know the sort of people that'd be there."

"I have listened to you several times in the past. You always ask these questions even though you know what the answers will be. The most important thing is that you're invited to the party. It doesn't matter if you know anyone."

I felt slightly guilty and humbled by Michelle's appraisal. She had a point. I had a way of projecting my humble background whenever there was a party in the offing, and at this moment, I wondered whether my past behavior was a reflection of my low self-esteem.

"I don't know. I guess... I feel I'd always be out of place."

"No. You shouldn't say that about yourself. You've done great for yourself. I was made partner in this company because of the influence of my father, but you've had to work your way through the process and ladder..."

"You are a great lawyer Michelle," I cut in. Michelle took a deep breath and took her hand from my shoulder.

"I know I'm a good lawyer, but I've had greatness thrust upon me. But not you. You fought hard to be here. You achieved greatness. You should be proud of yourself. Stop feeling so small."

"You think I feel small?" I asked.

Michelle walked closer towards me and gently pushed back the strands of hair that danced to the front of my face.

"Tell me, Sarah. What do you think?" She fixed her eyes on my face.

In the silence that prevailed between us, I was closeted in my mind. Voices, interpenetrating voices, collided as I tried to channel an appropriate response to Michelle's question.

Michelle's hand moved from my hair and settled on my shoulder. She rolled her hand from my shoulder and down to my right hand, taking a firm look at my light-coffee skin as she grabbed it.

"Your brown eyes are really beautiful when you're thoughtful," Michelle said softly.

"I guess you're mostly right about me. I recognize my abilities and hard work. But maybe if you were in my shoes, you'd have a better picture. I do not feel bad about my own accomplishments, but these parties expose the gap between the rich and poor... I'm still trying to get used to them."

"I understand. Inequality has always been a feature of the world. It has always been around, and I don't think it'd ever leave... But you can be better. You can be..." Michelle curled her hands around the nape of my neck and took a firm look at my face.

"You can still be beautiful, confident, and live a little in their midst. To be honest, most people would be humbled by your intelligence."

"You always know how to make me happy and confident."

"No. You are already happy and confident Sarah. I am just trying to stop you from being intimidated by the success of other people." She loosened her hands from the back of my neck, and walked back towards the window, leaning against it.

Slowly, I walked towards her, and for a brief moment I counted my blessings. When I started working in this company, Michelle came across as detached and supercilious. Although I had always admired her dress sense, I had convinced myself to keep my interactions with her strict and professional. It felt like I was having a culture shock when I was actually exposed to her cheerful, friendly side. Michelle initiated the process that had culminated into an enduring, loving friendship between us.

Michelle turned around and gazed out the window.

"It's a beautiful day Sarah. We better go shopping now. The party is on Saturday."

"Tomorrow??"

"You have somewhere to be?" she said, as she turned around and faced me.

"Not really, but shouldn't you have told me earlier?"

"I almost didn't want to go for the party, but my dad wants me to be there. You see, he's making inroads into the real estate industry. He needs men like Frank Steward on his side."

"So, it's business?"

"For them it is, but I can't be alone. If you have somewhere you'd rather be, I'll really understand."

I folded my hands across my stomach and backed away from her. I lived an introverted, private life. I was usually indoors and found comfort in bingeing on Netflix and reading books.

"Why are you so quiet?" Michelle asked.

"I'd like to come with you, but can you make up your mind quickly next time? Give me enough time to prepare for it?"

"I'm buying you a dress to make up for it."

"No. No..."

"Yes," Michelle insisted, closing in on me. "We are going shopping together. You're not just accompanying me."

I opened my mouth, willed to find an excuse to put her off her sudden benevolence, but I couldn't find the right word. Internally, I felt I needed a few new clothes. I had a lot of decent dresses, but I knew that the birthday party of Frank Steward would feature lots of extravagance, especially from ladies.

"I'll wait for you to pack up your things," Michelle added seriously.

She suddenly took a formal, business look that made me remember that she is the boss. She had already made up her mind to buy me a dress whether I liked it or not.

Our eyes locked for a moment.

"Come on. I'm waiting for you," Michelle said, walking towards the door. She opened the door and stood in the doorway.

Michelle was no longer smiling. She had an expressionless look that reminded me of the side of her that I had met at the start of my life at Hutchinson & Co Legal.

I pulled out the first drawer on my desk and dropped a file containing a deed of partnership in it.

I shut down my laptop, picked up my bag and looked up at Michelle. She was still in the doorway, retaining that serious look on her face.

"Ready?" She asked.

"Yeah."

A smile touched the corners of her lips. She nodded, losing the need to take a serious expression.

II

SARAH

We moved side by side through the hallway towards the elevator. The hallways were wide and ceilings high. Although the hallways were spacious, staff still kept a fair distance as they walked past us.

With every step, the sound of Michelle's heels echoed, demanding authority. Everyone looked up from their phones as they approached us, smiling in her direction. She let off a half smile, slightly pouting her red lips. She always had a way of showing power, yet her gentle side.

We were crammed in the elevator with two junior lawyers who were conversational and friendly with Michelle. It was easy to see that Michelle preferred to avoid such needless conversations, but the lawyers clearly intended to seize the opportunity to have a moment with her.

At the elevator lobby, Michelle weaved her hand around my shoulder endearingly. She detached herself from the lawyers who obviously intended to carryover their conversation into the lobby.

For a while, I wondered if Michelle endured the burden of being cheerful around people she would prefer to ignore. I wondered if her behavior was just a reflection of her business expectations.

I took a look over my shoulder and met the lawyers speaking in low tones as they stood a measured distance from the elevator.

The Hutchinson building was fourteen stories high with a large, sprawling parking lot.

I followed Michelle to her gray Cadillac. Michelle had access to other luxurious cars, but she preferred this one because it was gifted to her by her grandfather who died two weeks after her birthday. The coincidence had created an intrinsic value that Michelle couldn't resist.

Slowly, Michelle drove from the building and turned on the stereo. Moments later, she hurtled down the road, humming the song wafting up from the stereo.

"Do you think you have a responsibility to be nice to everyone in the company?" I asked.

"Yeah. I don't have to speak to anyone, but when I have to, I have to make them feel wanted and appreciated. My father has a funny way of saying it."

"I'd like to hear it."

"Nah. It's too cocky."

"Test me."

"Are you sure?"

"Yeah."

"Okay. Be charitable but stay away from the poor and needy. If you ever come across them, you have to make them feel that it is equally a privilege to be in their midst," Michelle said, and took a glimpse at me.

I took a deep breath and nodded. I wasn't surprised by this admonishment. It was necessary in a world where poor people saw the rich as an easy ticket away from their misery.

"Goddamn it," Michelle said, suddenly.

"I forgot my debit card."

"Oh."

"It's okay. I'll just drive home."

Michelle drove towards Ramona Gardens where she lived with her parents. She had a serious and angry look on her face and kept hissing as she kept her eyes on the road.

"I think you have to take it easy on yourself. You can easily get the card."

"I hate making silly, simple mistakes Sarah. I knew I was going shopping when I left home this morning. I shouldn't have forgotten the card."

"Mistakes happen."

"Yeah, but I don't like this kind of mistakes. It's a waste of my time."

III

Edmond

I decided to work from home today. Although I loved driving and the office wasn't far away, it had been a long week and I would rather save my energy for the busy weekend I had ahead.

I took my laptop out of my bag and sat at the edge of the bed, curious about the working day had in store. To my dismay, it was filled with a bunch of client meetings. I just wanted to sleep.

I closed my laptop and walked towards the bathroom. As I turned the shower knob, steam filled the bathroom. I walked towards the mirror and wiped it with the sleeve of my shirt. Although I could just about make out my face, it was obvious that I was in desperate need of a shave. Black stubble protruded from my chin. It felt rough and a little itchy.

A hot waterfall poured down on me as I entered the shower. I don't know why it felt so good, but it was always the simple things in life that gave me the most pleasure. The shower was my safe place, my place of freedom, a place where I could sing to my heart's content with no judgement or disturbance. It was a place with no pressure where my mind could freely run wild. I often got the best business ideas when I was in the shower.

Unfortunately, I knew I couldn't stay in here forever. I turned off the shower, wiped myself dry with a towel and got dressed. I chose a white shirt and denim blue jeans.

"What would you like to eat this morning?" Martha said, as I walked into the kitchen.

"My usual please," I responded. As I said, I am a simple guy.

Martha looked after everything in my house. The cooking, cleaning, shopping. She was honestly great, and I don't know what I would do without her.

Martha had been with me since I moved out of my father's house. She was an older woman, around 60 years of age, and was no more than 5'2 in height. She had dark brown hair which was always tied up into a slick bun. She was one of the most organized people I had ever met.

I made my way to my home office, set up my laptop and organized the documents that I needed for the day. A few moments later, there was a knock on the door.

"It's me Edmond." Martha had a British accent, and her voice was always soft and calm.

"Come in," I belted.

As she entered, the aroma of my breakfast and coffee filled the room. Martha dropped the tray of food to the side of my desk. It was eggs benedict and Martha's special recipe was far from simple. The two poached eggs sat perfectly on top of a strip of light brown bacon, which was perfectly balanced on top of a muffin. The hollandaise sauce dripped down the eggs, like molten lava which had overpoured onto the outside of a volcano. It was only on weekends and rare occasions when I worked from home during the week that I had time to eat breakfast.

"Mmm. Thanks Martha."

"Oo, you have a call coming in!" she exclaimed. "Have a lovely day, Edmond."

It was my father.

"Hi son. Do you have any plans for tomorrow night?"

IV
Sarah

Michelle's home was three stories high. The exterior was beige and there were brown cobbles laid across the ground all the way to the entrance of the door. At one side of the building, a large lawn was interspersed with differently shaped and well-trimmed plants. On the other side there was a swimming pool with several white lounge chairs at its side.

Michelle was relaxed and coordinated after alighting from her car. There was no sign of the pointless anger and frustration she momentarily displayed in the car.

It was the first time I was visiting her home, and I was instantly taken by the beauty weaved through it.

Together, we walked through the flight of stairs leading to the porch that led to the entrance door.

"You can wait here. I'll be right back," Michelle said, and hurried towards an elevator at the ground floor.

The ground floor was sprawling and decorated with luxurious features. It was easy to see that it was built as a banquet room. There were several clusters of couches on the floor, and also a slightly overhung platform at the top of the wall. The platform had several musical instruments.

I tried to hide my amusement of the finer things in life as I moved from the doorway and walked around the floor. The smell of lavender layered the atmosphere. As I gazed up, it was impossible to ignore the glass chandelier. It looked like it was formed of a thousand crystals and lit up every corner of the room. I found a couch to sit on as I continued to scan the house in awe.

The elevator door clicked open, and the towering frame of Hutchinson moved from it. Hutchinson was a bald-headed man with blue eyes and wrinkled brows. He walked majestically, a king in his palace.

He wore a navy-blue robe and held a golf club in one hand and a glass of wine in the other. His skin was oiled and shiny and the smell of his perfume wafted towards me.

Hutchinson didn't recognize my presence on the couch. He had his eyes on the golf course. Incidentally, my phone beeped. The sound sent a grim shiver up my spine.

Hutchinson turned towards me and took a studious look at me. He was quiet and watched me. In the persisting silence, I wondered if he had asked a question that my sudden rush of anxiety had made me miss.

I stood up quickly and almost fell back on the couch.

"I am...em...I am Sarah..."

"I remember you now. The supervisor, huh?" Hutchinson asked.

"Yeah. I'm the supervisor."

Hutchinson nodded and kept his eyes on me.

"What brings you to my place?"

"I came with Michelle."

"Oh... I see... What do you drink?"

"Michelle is... she is going to be right back."

Why was I so nervous to speak to someone I had exchanged emails with in the past?

Hutchinson nodded and took a sip of wine.

Incidentally, Michelle walked out from the elevator and drifted towards us.

"Dad?" she asked.

"You left your guest alone. That's not decent," Hutchinson responded.

"She hasn't come to see me. We're going shopping."

"Oh. All the best," Hutchinson said, managing a smile. Michelle turned towards me.

"Come on."

In the Cadillac, I became comfortable and introspective. Hutchinson offered a rare presence in the firm, which, in fairness, was now under the guidance of Michelle. I couldn't understand the fright that gripped me in his presence, but I had a sense that his calm and friendly behavior followed his usual practice of always making underprivileged people comfortable in his presence.

Michelle pulled up at Top Luxury in Santa Monica. It was a big boutique, adorned with glass doors that detected motion signals.

Inside the bouquet, we met Sally Hansen. Sally was an ebony woman with dark, locked hair and inky eyes. She had a dimpled smile on her face and embraced us with a hug.

"I was almost going to send a text Michelle. I've been waiting for you," Sally said with a smile.

"Yeah. I had to deal with a few issues on the way."

"That's alright. Come on. Let's not waste any time," Sally said infusing herself between Michelle and me. She placed her hands on our shoulders, endearingly, and led us towards a room at the end of the sprawling room.

The room had glass walls that made it slightly difficult to detect the right placement of the hangers and cabinets in the room.

"Michelle, I carefully selected these dresses for you." She picked out a few dresses from the hanger and dropped them on a couch at the side. Sally turned to me.

"Come Sarah. You have a perfect body," as she weaved her hand across my waist. "As soon as I received your picture from Michelle, I knew exactly what would fit you."

Sally led me to a hanger a few yards away and picked out several dresses.

"Try them on. I'll be right back."

I considered the dresses and knew at once that I wouldn't be able to afford them. They were beautiful, but I knew that Sally's preferential treatment towards us was anchored on Michelle's privilege and purchasing power.

All six dresses fitted perfectly, but I was slightly sad because I couldn't just pick one from the lot. I tried to restrain myself from being selfish and needy, but it was difficult to just accept the fact that I could only take one dress.

I dropped down on the couch, placed one hand on my cheek, and decidedly counted my blessings. This brief moment of introspection purged me of the sense of entailment that threatened to ruin my mood.

I reminded myself that I was privileged to be friends with Michelle. I was privileged to receive such a kind gesture from her.

Finally, I settled for a sequined, long black dress. The dress gently gripped me showing off my figure and had a halter neck with a high slit on the right side. It had a luxurious aura about it.

I stood from the chair and held the dress up before me. I embraced it and received a tap on my back. It was Michelle.

"What's up with you?" she asked.

"This dress is really beautiful."

"Oh. Have you tried the shoes?"

"The shoes? What shoes?"

Michelle shook her head and opened a small cabinet underneath the hanger. She brought out six shoes.

"These shoes?"

"Sally didn't tell me about shoes."

"I guess she has other business to attend to. Sometimes it makes them forgetful."

I nodded and picked up a black pair of high-heeled shoes. It was easy to see that it would gel smoothly with the black dress.

After putting on the shoes, I noticed that Michelle was opening another cabinet beside the first one. She brought out six bags.

I noticed that each bag was designed to match a combination of a dress and a pair of shoes.

"I need to ask you a question Michelle."

"What?"

"The shoes. I'm only taking one, right?"

"No. I paid for six."

"What? Is this a joke? Are you just… I mean…"

"I didn't want to tell you because I know you'd argue. I want you to have these dresses because there are lots of parties at this time of the year. I want you to look really nice and beautiful."

"You are paying for six dresses and shoes…"

"And bags," Michelle cut in, interrupting me.

"Why? What have I done to deserve this kindness?"

"You are a great friend Sarah. If I can't be kind to you, what kind of a friend am I?"

Michelle's words touched me and made me emotional. I blinked repeatedly, fighting the urge to resort to tears. I felt my eyes becoming wet, so I dropped my face.

I felt Michelle's hands on my shoulder.

"Sally is here. You don't want to cry in her presence," Michelle whispered.

I ran the back of my right hand through my eyes and raised up my face quickly. I feigned a smile and tried to put up a normal look.

Only, as I looked through the room, I discovered that Sally was not in the room. It was still just the two of us.

"I got you," Michelle said chuckling.

The smile on my face broadened as I watched her. I was half-confined in my mind. I knew that it wasn't easy to find a friend like Michelle. It wasn't easy to be so fortunate and blessed with a company that touched every segment of your life.

I was delighted and found a way to cling onto joy without resorting to tears. I picked up a purple dress, and as I regarded it, intently, I dropped it back on the couch, and charged at Michelle.

I gave her a tight, warm embrace, unwilling to let go. I was emotional again. Tears gathered in my eyes, but I was comforted by the realization that Michelle wouldn't be able to see them.

"Awwn. Look at this big baby," Michelle said, playing down the mood between us.

In any case, I knew she was affected by my behavior and emotional susceptibility to her kindness. The tone of her voice was tinged with emotion, and for a while I thought about looking into her eyes. I wanted to see if my exhibitions had rubbed off on her pleasantly.

When we drew apart, Michelle turned away from me. She brought out the rest of the bags from the cabinet, but I felt she was doing this to prevent me from seeing her eyes.

Incidentally, Sally returned to the room. She had a comforting smile and walked in calculated patters of feet.

"Tell me about the dresses, Sarah. Did everyone fit?"

"Yeah. They were perfect."

"Wow. I knew it. I have a model that has exactly your body size. You are more beautiful to be fair, but your hips and hers are just the same."

I blushed from Sally's compliment and received an insight into Sally's business sense. She had the ability to create the right impression and suffuse her clients with overwhelming confidence.

"Thank you," I responded.

"You didn't tell her about the bags and shoes?" Michelle asked.

"Oh! I didn't? My apologies. I must have assumed you were used to using our VIP room. My bad."

"It's alright. Hearing it from Michelle made it more worthwhile."

"If you don't mind, we have made some really nice cookies that will surely titillate your palates. I'm sure Michelle has told you about our cookies," Sally said excitedly. I turned to Michelle, who managed a smile and drew closer to me.

"I guess seeing is believing," Michelle responded.

Moments later, we moved to the waiting area of the boutique. It was set up like special restaurant. It had a large TV screen showcasing different fashion styles and red carpet designs.

We were entertained with cookies and cranberry juice. The cookies were delicious, but I was hardly occupied by its taste. I was thinking about my friendship with Michelle, which grew in beauty as if it had been ordained by God.

For a slight period, I wondered if I would be able to cope if Michelle suddenly decided to put an end to the friendship between us. The sadness that followed this thought left me with a jaded palate. It felt like I had received news of the death of a loved one.

Quickly, I shaved off this thought and took a gulp of cranberry juice. I looked up at Michelle and met her eyes. She had a faint smile on her face, but I couldn't genuinely match her smile.

I was shackled by a new kind of fear. Although I had stopped imagining her absence in my life, the fear that followed this thought remained.

"You are going to be so beautiful tomorrow evening," Michelle said, in a sibilant tone.

"I will try to keep up with your unmatchable beauty," I responded.

"Stop kidding yourself. You heard Sally, didn't you? You have a beauty that most can only get through the hands of a surgeon."

"Oh. Come on."

"Look at your cheeks and steeped face. I think you should look at the mirror often. Maybe you'll find the power that you possess."

Michelle took down her drink in two quick gulps and stood up.

"It's already dark. I have to drive you home."

I nodded, smiled, and mingled with other emotions I couldn't understand. I felt like a child having her first conscious experience of Christmas.

In the car, we were uncommunicative for a while. Michelle chose a Frank Sinatra song that impelled flashes of my moment with her in the Top Luxury. The delight I had experienced in the bouquet graduated back to the fore of my mind.

"Can I ask you a question?"

Michelle turned towards me, curiously.

"You already know you can ask me."

"Have you tried to move on from your last relationship? Have you tried to find someone else to love?" I asked.

Michelle exuded a faint, sad smile and turned back to the road.

"That experience broke me, Sarah. I thought he really loved me. I really couldn't accept that he wanted me for what he could get."

"But there are other great guys out there. You're so beautiful. If I were a guy, I would want to date you."

"Well, you are not a guy Sarah. And how I would I know that the next guy isn't trying to exploit me?"

"You may never really find love if you're afraid of getting your heart broken."

"Have you found love Sarah?"

"No. But I'm hoping I would. I'm opening my heart for an experience of love."

"Good for you. Since my last relationship, I've been asked out by a few decent men, but I don't think a relationship is right for me at this point. I want to create more friendships," Michelle said, taking a glimpse at me. "In the past, I underestimated the importance of having friends in my life. If I had a friend like you, I wouldn't have felt so miserable after I left him."

Michelle's words sent chilling flushes through my stomach. If I had any doubt about the importance of my friendship to her, Michelle had virtually erased them with her calm, emotional words.

"I understand. A woman like you deserves all the love in the world, Michelle."

Michelle pressed her lips together and took a deep breath.

"Sometimes, life is unfair to good people. I don't think this world is made for people with good intentions."

"No. Don't be like that. Lots of good people have found love and blessings from life," I responded.

"Yeah. Maybe. Some of us will never be lucky to enter the right relationship."

Michelle kept her eyes on the road. The tone of her voice was disturbing. She sounded like she was close to crying, but there was no sign of tears in her eyes.

I was filled with regret for bringing up this discussion. It would have been better to luxuriate in the blessings and pleasure of the day.

I sat back, short of words, and disturbed by Michelle's strange pessimism. Although I wasn't close to her during her last relationship, it was easy to see that one bad relationship can break a person to the point of no return.

"I really believe in you, Michelle. I really believe you'll find love, but I'll stop talking about it."

"No. It's okay. The past is in the past even though it affects the present sometimes."

We were uncommunicative through the rest of the journey. I couldn't focus on the delight of being blessed by Michelle because I was caught up in the pessimism that engulfed her belief in a loving relationship.

Michelle, surprisingly, looked away from me. She preferred to look towards the window at her side. I could see she was emotional and drawn to a past filled with heartbreak and treachery, but I could see her impressive desire to be strong before me.

Michelle pulled up at the periphery of my apartment building. She managed a smile, which had no trace of sincerity.

"I will come pick you up tomorrow by 7pm," Michelle said, smiling again. I nodded and smiled.

"You've been good to me, Michelle. You've been really good to me…"

"It's okay. It's just…"

"No. It's not okay. I want you to hear it, Michelle. I want you to see how grateful I am for having a friend like you. You are available to talk to. And you've done something for me that no one else has done. You're a great friend. You're the greatest friend I've had."

Michelle sniffled and pressed her lips together before exuding a smile that looked different and sincere.

"Thank you," she said.

"No. Thank you, Michelle. Thank you for today. Thank you for the sunshine you bring to my life every day."

Trickles of tears welled up in her eyes, but Michelle loomed her face down and took out her phone from her bag. She wiped her eyes as she pretended to be staring at something on her phone.

"Goodnight Michelle. Drive carefully," I said, opening the door.

"Goodnight," Michelle responded, looking up at me.

After alighting from the car, I opened the door to the backseat and took out my bags. Michelle had left hers in the trunk to make it easy for us to sort out.

As I held on to the three bags at periphery of my apartment building, I watched as Michelle turned back to the road. I maintained my position until she was out of my line of vision.

I moved towards the elevator lobby slowly. I lived in a room apartment on the seventh floor.

In the elevator lobby, I met a couple making out. They totally ignored my presence and continued with their lovemaking as I made my way to the elevator.

At the passageway of the seventh floor, I met another couple. The lady had one leg curled around the thigh of the man, who had her against the wall.

They stopped and separated once they heard the sound of my footsteps. I shook my head and continued forward. At the door of my apartment, I looked over my shoulder and discovered that the couple had continued from where they left off. There was obviously something in the air that impelled lovemaking around here.

I moved into my living room, dropped the bags in my bedroom and dropped down in the bed.

V

SARAH

Michelle chose a white dress for the party. It was sequined with shiny, sparkling pearls at her waist region. Her hair was tied in a bun, and she was incredibly beautiful.

Michelle leaned against her Cadillac and fixed her eyes on me as I walked towards her. I was comfortable in my dress, and my sense of belonging increased in this outfit.

The dress, it seemed, created the impetus to gain the required attitude for this meeting. Two yards away from Michelle, I stopped abruptly and took a long look at my dress and the black pump shoes that gelled perfectly with it. I had equally chosen a black bag.

"I didn't think you'd choose the black dress," Michelle said, with a bold, big smile.

"What is wrong with it?"

"Nothing. Nothing at all. You're so beautiful, Sarah. You'll catch many eyes."

"Is that a good thing?"

"It depends on what you want," Michelle said, embracing me.

I was slightly uncomfortable after Michelle's utterance. I wondered if I had somehow chosen the wrong combination of color. I wondered whether this all-black outfit had a mournful aura in spite of its beauty.

In the car, Michelle chose a rock song and kept the volume loud, stifling any chance of a conversation with her.

She was happy and to be fair, it made me happy. I had wondered whether the negative influence of our conversation the previous night would be detectable in her behavior today.

In any case, this was a version of Michelle I had hoped to see. Hence, the reservations I had about my dress quickly became secondary in the scheme of things.

After driving for a little more than nine minutes, Michelle pulled up outside the home of Frank Steward in Monterey Hills.

Two security personnel quickly hurried down to the Cadillac and backed off after recognizing Michelle.

"Do you think my dress is really good?" I asked.

"Of course. It's beautiful and confident. I'm sure it would have more influence on the perception of others about you."

"What do you mean?"

"This exudes class, Sarah. I'm sure you can see it already. Come on. Let's go."

Frank Steward's house had uncanny similarity with the home of Michelle. It was a three storied building and had the same façade with the home of Michelle. Only, there was no sign of a sprawling lawn or pool at the sides of the building. There was a basketball court on one side, and it was the only recreational facility outside the building. The building had more parking space than most restaurants and bars in LA.

We met another coterie of security personnel at the entrance door of the house. They took a look at Michelle's face, bowed, and opened the door.

We were introduced to the sound of music. It was a calming rendition that announced the mood of the party. There was a pianist, a violinist, and two guitarists at the top of the floor.

After taking a quick look through the floor, I had a strong conviction that the home of Michelle had been designed by the same architect.

I met Hutchinson beside a wall, drained in a conversation with a gentleman. The gentleman had short auburn hair and looked interested in the conversation with Hutchinson.

"That's Frank Steward," Michelle muttered.

"He is so hot," I replied.

"Yeah. You're right."

Michelle replied without turning towards me. She had her eyes on Frank Steward, and she had a look that gave me the immediate impression that she was into him.

In the transitory moment of silence between us, Michelle was lost in her gaze at him. I was happy and concerned at the same time. I was happy that her previous nightmare hadn't instigated a total shutdown on the chances of opening up her heart to a lover.

Also, I was concerned because Michelle didn't exude the excitement that gripped a lady caught up in a spell of admiration and love for a man. There were scrims of fear in her eyes.

There were several tray-wielding stewards on the ground floor and glasses of Champagne on the trays. I moved towards a steward and picked out two glasses of Champagne.

Afterwards, I nudged Michelle, who smiled as she turned towards me.

"Thank you," Michelle said, taking a glass from my hand.

"I hope you are fine."

"Of course. I am fine. Come on. Let's go inside."

I walked beside her and followed her to a couch.

There were only about forty guests on the ground floor. It was easy to see that Frank Steward kept his circle small.

Michelle looked over her shoulder at the part of the wall she had met Hutchinson and Steward.

"You like him?" I asked.

Michelle turned toward me and shook her head. I didn't understand the look on her face, but it appeared she didn't like the fact that I was trying to demystify her gaze at Steward.

"I am just wondering what my dad is saying to him."

"Real estate? You said your dad is making an entry, didn't you?"

"Yeah, but they look really excited to speak to each other. Don't you see that?" Michelle asked.

I nodded and took a sip of Champagne.

I watched some of the guests as they exchanged pleasantries. They kissed cheeks, embraced, and spoke decorously.

There was no scantily clad lady in the room. Every lady wore a dress and went for simple luxury.

Michelle and I exchanged pleasantries with two old ladies who treated me respectably as if they knew me before today. They didn't ask for my name, but they were full of compliments for my dress.

"Why do I have a feeling that they don't really care about our dresses?" I asked.

Michelle smiled and took a gulp of Champagne.

"You are finally getting it," Michelle responded.

"Getting what?"

"No one really cares. Everyone tries to look good and cheerful because you don't know who your next business partner would be."

"That's interesting."

"I'll be right back," Michelle said, standing up from the couch.

She moved towards Hutchinson, who had finished speaking with Steward. Steward was on his way to the overhung platform. He shook a few hands and embraced a few persons.

At the platform, he took a mic and formally welcomed everyone to his birthday party. He held forth, impressively, about his life as a boy, and how he had always nurtured the dream of standing before these fine people celebrating him.

The end of his speech was marked by a rapturous applause. Some of the guests stood up from their chairs and clapped. I kept an eye on Michelle, who was still huddled up with her father.

At the end of the applause, Steward invited Shirley Temple, a prominent country singer on stage. I didn't know Shirley was on the ground floor. She was popular, and in any other occasion, there would have been a throng of people jostling for her autograph.

Seeing Shirley Temple on stage sent chilling flushes through my stomach. Her entrance was graced by an applause, but it was an applause that followed a formal route. It didn't show any real excitement from the guests, who went back to holding soft, measured conversations.

When Shirley started singing, the conversing voices gradually tapered off until everyone was attentive to Shirley's rendition.

Hutchinson and Michelle were still standing together, but Michelle fixed her eyes on Shirley.

I had listened to this particular song several times and understood the influence it had on the guests. I had been in this situation several times, and it wasn't just because of her wonderful voice. Shirley understood how poetry could be the oil with which true relationship was eaten.

Towards the end of the rendition, I met the eyes of a gorgeous man on a couch beside me. He was sitting alone and looked towards me from the brim of his glass.

He had sexy, piercing grey eyes that had been cooked in a pot of enchantment. I couldn't stand the look in his eyes or the messages they silently conveyed.

He wore a grey suit, and his black hair was low trimmed. His chin was clean-shaven and steeped, and just before I took my eyes from him, he took a sip of Champagne from his glass.

It was the sexiest display I had seen in a long time. The mundane task of drinking Champagne hadn't ever had such a compelling influence on me. I had to turn towards him, wholeheartedly missing out on the closing lyrics of Shirley's rendition.

The brim of the glass was trapped between his lips as he kept his eyes on me. He looked like a vampire from one of those Netflix movies I usually watched at night. He looked like the kind of vampire that was lonely and had the desire to turn me into a vampire so that I would be interminably stuck with him.

The sound of Shirley's voice jerked me off the mesmerism that came from this man's attention. I kept my eyes on Shirley without truly listening to her.

I felt the stabbing impulse to turn towards the grey-eyed sorcerer, who had effectively left his spell on me. I resisted this urge and kept my eyes on Shirley even though it meant I wouldn't be able to enjoy her rendition.

I was mostly confined in my mind and gripped by my own imaginations. I had a mind that had the alluring, funny ability to conjure up the most fascinating imaginations. As I kept my eyes on Shirley, I received imagined flashes of myself walking down the aisle, laced in a beautiful wedding dress.

I couldn't shut out this thought because my mind found it appealing, and internally I flirted with the idea.

Perhaps as always, I had become a character in my own mind. It was not the first time I had been entrapped in a vivid imagination. My mind had the unique quality of springing up these masterpieces irrespective of the situation.

Perhaps that was the reason why I was working on a novel. It was the perfect place for me to leave reality and throw my imaginations.

As if to feed my mind with more weapons, this handsome gentleman moved from his seat in the middle of the rendition. Although I kept my eyes on Shirley, the rest of my senses heightened and were purely focused on him. He dropped down beside me and sent a shiver up my spine.

He was quiet for a moment. A pulse tapped away on my right wrist as I pretended not to notice his presence at my side.

I was waiting for his words. I wanted to listen to him, and in spite of my love for Shirley, my thoughts drowned out every other sound in the room. Who would have thought that the silence of a gentleman would overshadow the thrilling voice and rendition of Shirley Temple?

"Do you know what's more impressive about seeing you?" he asked. I turned towards him and tried to put on a perplexed expression.

"Are you speaking to me?"

"Yes. But you already know that."

"Shirley is a great singer," I said, glibly.

"I have her songs at home. I can listen to her whenever I want. But not you. You are an enigma that I don't intend to crack."

"I don't understand."

"I don't understand myself. But what's more impressive is that as soon as I saw you, I started to understand what it means to fall in love at first sight."

"You are kidding," I said, surprised by his choice of words.

"Kidding. I wish I was. I see a home in your eyes, Miss…"

He was quiet and expectant. Our eyes locked as he waited for me to say my name.

"Sarah… Sarah Barry," I said finally.

"I'm Edmond. Edmond Barker."

He kept his eyes on me and became momentarily quiet. I couldn't turn away from him. I didn't want to. Edmond had an appealing smell and a face that was fit for most romance movies.

"Don't you see something Sarah?"

"What?"

"Don't you see we are about to walk on the edge of something amazing?"

"I am not sure I understand…I don't…"

"It's okay. We do not always find the right words in the most interesting times. You're the confirmation of so many beautiful feelings."

"Have we met before?"

"No. That is why this is so beautiful. It feels like I've known you all my life."

"I see. You're assuming that I'm single."

Edmond smiled and exposed his incisors briefly.

"I know you're single. If you're not, then you have to be trapped in a situation you need to exit."

"Why would you think so?"

"Because this feeling wouldn't come if the situation wasn't right."

"I see you respect coincidences, but I'm..."

"Be sincere with me Sarah. Look into my eyes."

I refused to look into his eyes because I knew it would easily make me powerless before him. There was something in his eyes that I couldn't understand.

Edmond placed his two fingers on my chin and raised my face up, ensuring our eyes were locked. His grey eyes were studious, and his lips were wet with Champagne.

"What do you see?" he asked, with an air of authority.

"I don't know. I'm not sure."

"What do you feel?"

"I can't say."

"Tell me."

I took a deep breath and wondered if Edmond had truly cast a spell on me. The authority in his voice was supposed to put me off, but I found myself falling harder for him.

"You are handsome, but I..."

A round of applause swept through the room. I had completely forgotten where I was. I found stability and organization in my thought and tried to cling onto the distraction around me.

I looked over my shoulder, but there was no sign of Michelle and Hutchinson. I was alone.

"Are you afraid?" Edmond asked.

"No."

"I think I understand how you feel."

"How do I feel?"

"You didn't think it would ever be like this. You didn't think you'd find love this way. You see it in books and movies, but it isn't supposed to be real."

"It is a bit crazy to be honest. I think you're a handsome man, but sometimes first appearances can be deceiving."

"You're talking to a guy that doesn't believe in love at first sight until today. My experiences and perceptions are being quenched by my sudden feelings for you." He slowly lowered his hands and placed it on his thigh. "Just tell me you didn't feel anything. I'll not bother you again."

I took a deep breath and looked into his eyes where the enchantment lay. I knew it was going to be a terrible mistake to resort to lies in this situation. Edmond was a serious man that had decided to wear his feelings on his sleeves.

"I feel something. I was…I liked… I wanted to look at you. I really wanted to look at you," I replied, mingling with intense palpitations.

Warm fluids flitted through my stomach. Expressing my immediate feelings before him made me anxious.

Edmond took a sip of Champagne without taking his eyes from mine.

"I was right. We are about to walk on the edge of something beautiful."

"Why does this feel like a dream? Why does it feel like you're unserious and playing a game?"

"The best feelings come that way. Want to take a stroll?" Edmond asked, standing up from the couch. His question suddenly didn't feel like a question as he stretched his hand towards me.

I took his hand without responding to his question. As our fingers interlinked, I felt the warmth of his body. His hands were large and wrapped around mine like a baby in a blanket. We walked outside the house and strolled to the basketball court at the side.

There was a well-manicured line of grass at both sides of the court and a gibbous moon in the sky.

For some reason I was comfortable, yet so uncomfortable at the same time. I was walking with a stranger I had only just met, but Edmond didn't feel like a stranger. Edmond felt like the answer to the wishes and imaginations that had gripped many lonely nights. It seemed he was the universe's way of indicating that it had always listened to the yearnings of my heart.

"What's next Edmond?" I asked.

Edmond stopped abruptly and turned towards me.

"Please, call me Ed, but that's a very good question. We should exchange contacts first," he said with a big smile.

Edmond took my hand again and led me away from the court. We were back to the front of the building, but Edmond started towards the parking lot.

He led me to a Mustang, opened the door, and turned towards me.

"I want to give you something of me."

"Something of you?"

"Yeah. Something that easily reminds you of me."

"Why? Are you going to be away for a long time?"

"No. Not at all. Take it as my first romantic gesture towards you."

Edmond climbed into the car, opened the dashboard, and returned with a wristwatch on a glass casing.

He brought out the wristwatch and weaved it across my hand. It was a silver, feminine wristwatch and although I thought it was beautiful, I wondered why he had a feminine wristwatch in his dashboard.

"This is so beautiful. Do you really think you should be giving this to me?"

"I have no doubt. I have no doubt at all. This is a reflection of how much I trust my feelings for you."

He weaved his hand around my wrist and drew closer. I couldn't see his eyes clearly in the dark, but Edmond had done enough to keep my mind occupied.

"What's on your mind?"

"It still feels like a dream?"

"Would a kiss solve that?"

"I don't know."

Edmond leaned closer and left a kiss on my cheek. Once his lips touched my cheek, I felt a vibration inside me. It was a terrible, eerie vibration that swept through my body and settled on my privates, exposing my rampaging horniness and lack of sex.

I was stabbed by the desire to kiss his lips as he took them from my cheek, but I managed to stave off this impulse with great difficulty. The vibration didn't stop and the desire to kiss him held me bound.

"How does it feel now?"

"So real," I whispered, wishing he would draw closer and kiss me again.

He stood a yard away and held my hand, raising it to his lips. He left a kiss on the back of my hand and squeezed his hand around my wrist.

"We should go inside now," he said, in a sibilant tone.

As he took a step forward, I couldn't move my legs. I didn't want to go back inside. At least not yet. Edmond's presence around me had soaked off the allures of the party.

Edmond turned around, noticing my reluctance. He was apt and drew closer without asking any question. He embraced me, weaving his hands around my waist.

It was at this moment it actually hit me. The reality of my time with Edmond became more vivid. I marveled at the indication that I was willing to be lost in the love of a man that I barely knew.

The power of love was, at once, reified before my eyes. Nothing else would have had such glaring influence on me. I was confined In a thought process that prioritized a feeling that was nonexistent two hours ago.

It was funny, strange, and I had a vivid sense of the absurdity of love at first sight. The way my sense of reason fizzled out, the way the vestigial traces of paranoia was unwilling to interfere in a feeling that rendered me powerless, the way I was willing to be alone with Edmond at the parking lot.

Edmond left another kiss on my cheek and gradually took his lips to a corner of my lips. I quickly kissed his lips, seizing the opportunity and lowering my guards.

I was at the point where I was no longer willing to fight my feelings for him, and the passion and effort he put into the kiss showed that his thoughts aligned with mine.

Edmond was desperate to kiss me, and once I started off the kiss, he took charge and tightened his grip on my waist.

It was a long kiss that was apparently short in the timeline of my feelings. When our lips parted, my eyes were barely open. I wanted more of his succulent lips and the taste of champagne on them.

He placed his hands on my shoulder and kept his face inches away from mine. I could hear the sound of his breath. I could feel him passionately, as if he was inside me, and giving me the best sexual experience of my life.

It was the first time I was exposed to a nonsexual moment that surpassed the beauty of sex, and in the persisting silence, we maintained eye contact. I wanted to speak, but I didn't think it would make any sense. Most of the things I wanted to say were already documented in my eyes.

Given my brief knowledge of him, I knew Edmond already had a sense of my feelings for him. He seemed like the kind of guy that detected the subtleties that most would take for granted.

He took my hand again and turned toward the building. Without resorting to words, we started towards the building.

I mingled with feelings that were surreal and novel. There was no previous intimation of the sort of romance I had just experienced with him.

The guests were dancing when we returned to the ground floor. It created another opportunity for a romantic moment between us.

I detected compatibility in our movements. It was a slow dance, but our feet and movements were aligned.

His eyes were constricted and interlaced with a mesmerism that showed his smooth reciprocation of the feelings that flitted through my heart.

He kissed me, choosing my cheek in the presence of the guests. It was the end of the dance, and as I looked over my shoulder, I met Michelle. She had been dancing with Steward.

Michelle was looking in my direction. She was clearly surprised, and I totally understood her feelings. I was more impressed by the look in Steward's eyes. He was looking at Michelle's cleavage.

Michelle whispered something to him and walked towards me.

"Michelle brought me here. You know her right?" I asked, turning towards Edmond.

"Yeah. I saw you two together."

Michelle came before us and oscillated her gaze between Edmond and me.

"Edmond. I see you've made acquaintance with my friend," Michelle said softly.

"I have passed that stage Michelle. Sarah Barry lights up a protracted darkness inside me. She'll fill you in," Edmond said, leaving a kiss on my cheek. "I'll call you," he whispered, and started away from us.

Michelle stood before me as we kept our eyes on the departing frame of Edmond. I didn't want him to leave, but I was compensated by the knowledge that everything would not happen at once.

Michelle remained quiet and thoughtful after Edmond left the ground floor. She kept her eyes on the door and pressed her lips together.

"Is there a problem?" I asked. Michelle turned toward me and saw the silver wristwatch on my wrist.

"He gave this to you?"

"Yeah."

"He is supposed to be with Linda Evans."

"Who is Linda Evans?"

Michelle took a keen look at my face. I had become an open book. It was easy to think that Michelle was able to gauge my desperation to know more about Edmond.

"Just tell me what he said to you."

"I love him, Michelle, and he loves me too."

Michelle was shocked.

"Wow," Michelle said, dilating her eyes. She opened her mouth to say something but closed it back.

"Why aren't you saying anything Michelle?"

I was nervous and started to think that Edmond might have played me. He might have chosen a script and adhered religiously to it.

"Say something Michelle."

"Edmond has always been with Linda. For a long time, Linda has always been in the picture. They go to parties together. Everyone knows that."

"What does this mean?" I asked.

"Edmond comes across as a decent guy. His father is a top player in the real estate industry."

"What does this mean?"

"Maybe they are no longer together. It's a possibility."

"It has to be," I replied. "Maybe that's why he said I light up a protracted darkness inside him."

I was desperate. This was supposed to be a love story without distortions. Edmond was supposed to belong to me by virtue of his preachments. I was reminded of the compelling words he had used in initiating the romance between us. He believed I needed to be single for our relationship and the situation that brought us together to be perfect.

Michelle had a doubtful, concerned look, but she was careful not to make any aggravating utterance. She preferred to be quiet as she watched me.

"Are you going to be alright?" she asked.

I didn't know how to answer her question. I had just been exposed to an unprecedented romance that was suddenly threatened by a certain Linda Evans.

"He gave me this wristwatch because he wanted me to have something of him."

Michelle took another thoughtful look at the wristwatch.

"It is new. Who could he have bought it for?"

"You think he bought it for Linda?" I asked.

"Maybe. Maybe he bought it before they broke up. I think that makes sense," Michelle retorted.

Her words brought an uncanny equanimity to my mind. I believed those words. I believed Edmond broke up with Linda before he was able to hand her this wristwatch. Why would he give me such an expensive gift if he didn't trust his feelings for me?

Buoyed by emotion, I embraced Michelle and tightened my hands at her back. She drew apart from me quickly and placed her hands on my cheeks. Michelle continued to exude a concerned look.

She looked like an experienced woman, who was familiar with the situation that I found myself.

"Do not think about this Sarah. Trust me. It won't solve anything. You have to go with the flow. If you believe in this, you have to continue to believe until you don't have to."

I nodded, halfheartedly. Although her words were wise, I knew I wouldn't be able to stop myself from thinking about it. I was already thinking about getting information on Linda Evans.

"Are you listening to me?" Michelle asked.

"Yeah. I can hear you loud and clear."

"I'm going to confirm the situation between Edmond and Linda and get back to you."

"Thank you so much."

Michelle wasn't impressed by the look in my eyes. She saw through my lame show of strength.

"I'll drive you home. I need to tell Steward that we're leaving," Michelle said, stroking my hair slightly.

She took two steps on her back before turning away from me, sashaying towards Steward who was having a conversation with three men.

The presence of Michelle brought an abrupt end to their conversation. Steward focused on Michelle and moved away with her.

I thought Steward's move indicated his interest in Michelle. They were conversational and it actually gladdened my heart.

I sat on the nearest couch and waited for Michelle. I prevented myself from dwelling on the new information about Edmond's relationship with Linda. Instead, I focused on the romance I enjoyed with him.

I believed we were inextricable while the romance lasted. I took a glimpse at the wristwatch and started to have a sense of the motive of Edmond. Perhaps he had expected this doubt to arise after I had received information about his relationship with Linda. Perhaps he was in love with me too...

I had a strong conviction that he gifted me this wristwatch to remind me of his genuine interest in me.

Steward and Michelle walked towards me. They didn't hold hands or give off any hint of a persisting relationship between them.

"Thanks for providing such a great company for Michelle," Steward said suddenly.

"The pleasure is mine Sir. I'll forever be grateful for meeting her."

Steward and Michelle exchanged quick glances.

"Goodnight," Steward said, giving Michelle a warm embrace.

In the car, Michelle decided not to turn on the stereo. Silence in a night ride offered a conducive ambiance.

"I like the way Steward looks at you," I said suddenly.

"Don't count on it. We've been childhood friends. It is easy to mistake it for romance."

"Maybe that's what's blinding you from seeing what he feels for you."

"If he feels anything for me, he'd say it. I've seen enough to know that making assumptions can be dangerous."

Michelle had a serious look as she turned towards me. I became quiet again.

"I hope you won't be bothered about Linda?"

"Should I?"

"I don't think you should. At least you just met him. If he's still with Linda, it'll be easy to leave him and move on."

Although Michelle's words made sense, it exposed her inability to capture the effect of love at first sight. I knew after her words that she wouldn't be able to understand that Edmond had left a strong impression on me in one night.

How could I make Michelle understand that I had thought about spending the rest of my life with someone I had just met? How could I make her understand that it wouldn't be so easy to suddenly detach myself from him and forsake the imaginations he had impelled in my mind?

"I have a strong feeling they've broken up," I said finally.

"Feelings are great Sarah, but we still need to know the truth of the matter. The truth will put things in a better perspective."

VI
SARAH

It had been seven days since the birthday celebration of Frank Steward. Everything that had happened since then had fallen short of my expectation. I was supposed to be huddled up with Edmond, stitching out more romantic scenes.

Only, now, it felt like a long time ago. Edmond didn't call that night and he hadn't reached out since then.

I was alone in my office. I was supposed to be on way home, but I was in a terrible place. I didn't want to be sad, but I couldn't really find joy in the little things anymore.

I was stuck in indifference. The kind that made a person expressionless and detached from the beauty of the world around them.

I had, on each day, regarded the phone number of Edmond. I had thought about calling him, but it felt out of place. It didn't feel right to call a man that had indicated that he'd reach out to you.

I couldn't find an excuse to explain Edmond's behavior. I didn't think anyone could be so busy. If Edmond truly loved me, he should have found a way to reach out to me.

What if he lost his phone?

What if I typed in my number incorrectly?

I stood up from my chair and moved to the window. Everything down the road looked small from the fourteenth floor. If Edmond had lost his phone, he would have reached out to Michelle. There was no excuse.

I thought about Linda Evans. I had hindered the impulse to find information about her. And since Michelle was mostly busy this week, I couldn't get an opportunity to determine the current status of Edmond's relationship with Linda.

I had worn the silver wristwatch to work every day since the day I met him, except today. I started to feel a certain weakness inside me, as if it was all a horrible game and I was on the losing team. Did he ever feel the way I felt about him? Was this all a dream?

I took the wristwatch out of the top drawer of my office desk and held it carefully in the palm of my hand. It was like a portal to a whole new world, except Edmond held the key. I followed the movement of the second hand and was suddenly occupied by the memories of my time with Edmond.

The memories came slowly, in snatches, until they occupied every fragment of my mind.

I staggered from the window, emotional and sad. Tears gathered in my eyes, and it started to feel like I was on the verge of letting go. I walked back to my desk, picked up my bag, and dropped the wristwatch inside.

It was just past 6:50pm when I arrived home. I made myself a bowl of cereal and filled it with milk.

I turned on the TV and tried to continue a movie I couldn't finish the previous night. I couldn't believe how much Edmond had occupied my mind and life after only a few hours of being with him.

I ate the cereal halfway and contended with a jaded palate. This night was taking a trajectory that smelt like depression.

I had already been sad as a result of Edmond's continued silence, but the sadness I currently felt was different. It was the kind that lacked intensity but engulfed every bit of my life. It was the kind that drained me of joy without pushing me to tears. It was characterized by a rampaging sequence of indifference that seemed to fester every single day.

I dropped the bowl on the table and sat back on the couch. I tilted my face up and didn't know what to think about.

I had a shortage of pleasurable memories. If I took out the pleasures of spending time with Michelle, there was hardly anything else left. What on earth was going on?

I left the living room and proceeded to my bedroom. I threw myself into my beanbag which was located right next to my reading desk.

I unlocked my phone and looked at Edmond's phone number intently. I struggled to find the confidence to give him a call.

The Edmond I had seen at the party wouldn't just decide against calling me unless he had a good reason. After all, he did tell me he was going to give me a call.

Perhaps I had been wrong all along. Perhaps Edmond was still attached to Linda. Perhaps the experience I shared with him was the motivation he needed to go back to her. Perhaps I was just a pathway, a road, where people like Edmond received the therapy they needed to fully embrace their past.

All sorts of thoughts ran through my mind. It was terrible, but at least my eyes were clear. Internally, I knew my assessment was harsh and unfair, but logic wasn't enough to stop me.

I dropped my phone heavily on the floor, got up and sat at my desk to open my laptop. Since I was sad and crestfallen, I knew I was in a great mood to work on my novel.

Sadness was an important ingredient in writing. I didn't understand the process, but sadness had a way of refining my imagination and sharpening my muse.

Since I couldn't be with Edmond, I could at least use the emotion productively.

My novel was a fantasy romance. I wanted to create a world where death wasn't just a passage towards obscurity. In this novel, I created a beautiful country where the dead lived. A country that was accessible to the living three times a year. In those days, at least, the dead and the living could coexist and share memories and histories. I wanted to create a world where the power of death was diminished. A world where living was eternal, but most importantly, I wanted to create a story where death was unable to stop two lovers.

VII
EDMOND

I loved my mustang, but I had never won any racing game with it since purchasing it in September.

The other contestants had Ferraris and Porches, but I had a sneaky feeling that today would be perfect for my mustang.

The Blinks Center in Pacific Palisades offered a privileged, private enjoyment. It was only open to members and everyone of us coughed out $7,000 every month.

The winner of today's contest was entitled to a $100,000 prize. All 10 contestants placed a bet of $10,000 each. Last week, the best was $7,000. The week before, it was $5,000.

The racing game was becoming increasingly competitive, but I didn't really care about the money. I just wanted to experience the feeling of winning again. It had been a long time. Actually, I hadn't won a game since I broke up with Linda.

Linda was standing at the roadside, drinking from a glass of wine. I met her eyes a few times. There was nonchalance in those eyes.

As I opened my car and moved inside, she grimaced at me and stuck out her tongue mockingly.

Linda was a fine lady. She had a great, slim body, and long brunette hair. She was tall and equipped with features that would attract any man, but I couldn't stand her these days.

Since we broke up, it had become harder to believe that I had managed to cope with her baggage.

Linda was still looking at me from the side. It appeared she intended to do everything to make sure I didn't come out victorious. Her tongue was still jutted out of her mouth and her eyes were dilated.

Ahead, a coterie of six cheerleaders held on the prize money, which was crammed in a small glass box. The cheerleaders passed the box around and danced to the pervading music.

The umpire shot his gun and started off the race. I was half-closeted in my head, but I kept my eyes on the road. I tried to focus. I wanted to win.

There was Jayden, a swarthy, brawny guy, who was a reckless driver. Jayden was ahead, and he drove recklessly to keep everyone away from him.

There was my best friend, Kane. Kane was a great driver and had actually won the racing contest the previous week. Kane was athletic, white, focused, and intelligent.

There was also Smith, who had never won a race, but had been first runner-up for most of the races. Smith was white, had a solid frame, and worked as an investment banker.

I was closing in on Jayden, but I knew he had eyes on me. As I drew closer to him, he swerved towards me. It was a move I expected. I applied my brakes and sent him swerving to a corner.

We were already on the last lap. The unproductive move of Jayden put Kane in front and Smith just behind him.

Jayden and I were both in fifth and sixth place, respectively. It was a terrible move, but I could have been worse off if I had fallen for his tricks.

Kane came out on top again. He jumped onto the top of his car, opened a bottle of champagne to celebrate his win.

Linda stood beside his car and celebrated with him. Linda was really happy for him. She drank from his bottle of champagne and climbed up the top of the car to meet him. They embraced like a couple.

I was disappointed by this move, but I was hardly offended. Kane and Linda had been close friends before we started dating.

The cheerleaders handed the prize to Kane, who took several snapshots with them. The rest of the drivers started sending their congratulations and took pictures with Kane.

Jayden was beside me. He was disappointed and had a glare in his eyes as he regarded me. Suddenly, he moved from his car and charged towards me.

"I know what you did," Jayden said.

"What did I do?"

"You conspired with Kane, right? You guys are best friends. This will not happen next time."

Jayden waited for a response, but I had nothing to tell him. I could easily be pissed off with him for his reckless driving, but silence in this circumstance was more productive.

After waiting for some time for a response, he walked towards Kane and congratulated him without taking pictures with him.

Moments later, Kane turned towards me. Linda was still all over him. She was incredibly excited, but I already knew the game she was playing.

She was desperate for me to see her happy without me. And as if to reiterate my point, Linda turned towards me and stuck out her tongue as she took another snapshot with Kane.

After the photography session, Kane walked towards me with his prize money. I was sitting in my mustang, drinking from a bottle of water.

"You didn't want to take pictures with me?" Kane asked.

"Not with her around you."

"I hope you don't blame me for it. Linda and I have been…"

"Friends before I dated her. I know Kane. You don't have to say it every time."

"I actually feel bad right now. You don't look happy Ed."

"I'm happy you won. That's the most important thing."

"Linda is always going to be around. If you can't get over her, you should go back to her. I think you guys look great together."

"You want to know the truth Kane?"

"Yeah."

"She is not the problem right now. She is exploiting you. She is going to try to be more around you and deprive me from your friendship. Linda loves to divide and conquer."

"I feel you're overthinking this. Linda has always been like this. She has always been the life of the party."

"But she hasn't always been around you bro. What has changed?"

"I don't really see any changes. Just cheer up. If you want to move on from her, you have to stop caring about what she does."

Moments later, I was in the bathroom. It was a hot, therapeutic bath, despite that I could I hear the sound of moaning from nearby bathroom stalls. Some of the guys preferred to take a bath with their girlfriend, and sometimes they did more than just take a bath.

I was relaxed in the bathroom. I was thinking about Sarah Barry. I had a feeling she hated the way I had handled my appearance in her life.

I had fallen away from the promises I had made on the first day, but it was not because my feelings for her had suddenly disappeared.

I heard footsteps outside the hallway and the sound of whispers. *Was that Linda?* Quickly, I wrapped a towel around my waist and opened the door.

I took a quick look at the passageway. It was another lady and her boyfriend. They gave me a concerned look, but I quickly tucked back into the bathroom and continued my bath.

I spent another twenty minutes in the bathroom before I went to the lounge where Smith and Kane were having a drink.

There was wine, strawberries, and other fruits on the table. Thankfully, Linda was not with them.

As I made my way to the table, I felt bad about the power Linda had over me. If I was no longer in a relationship with her, why was I so worried about who she was hanging out with?

Kane filled an empty glass to the brim and handed it to me.

"Are you alright bro?"

I took the drink without responding to his question and sat back in the chair.

"Why do I have a feeling there's something you want to talk about?" Smith asked, focused on me.

"There is nothing important. This is something I have to resolve on my own."

"Resolve?" Smith asked, befuddled. "We resolve issues together, Ed. That's why we are friends."

"I hope this is not about Linda again?" Kane asked.

I took a gulp of wine and looked through the lounge. This building overlooked the racing tracks. There were other massive buildings around the Blinks Center, but the racers preferred to hang out here.

The other racers and their close friends were scattered around the other tables. It was a large room, but Linda was clearly absent.

"Where has she gone to?" I asked.

"I knew it. This is about Linda?" Kane retorted.

"Why have you chosen to suffer? Why did you decide to just break up with her? You guys looked great together," Smith added.

"Ed can be crazy sometimes. Sometimes his own philosophy gets the better of him," Kane added.

"It is over between the two of us. Why can't you guys just understand that?"

"It is not us that is the problem. You're the one always bringing her in our conversations," Kane responded.

I snuck a sip of wine and sat up in my chair.

"I have met another lady. She is so beautiful. I think I have fallen in love with her."

"Who is she?" Smith asked.

"Her name is Sarah Barry."

"Sarah Barry? It doesn't ring a bell at all. What business is her family into?" Kane asked.

I took a deep breath and took another gulp of wine. This time, I placed the glass on the table and rubbed my palms together.

"She is just a normal girl."

"Just a normal girl? She is poor?" Smith asked.

"No. She is okay. Just a normal girl."

Kane pressed his lips together and shook his head. He exhaled loudly, ushering in a moment of silence at the table.

Smith and Kane were ponderous and half-dampened by this news.

"You guys are overthinking this," I said softly.

"You know your family will not accept that. You're an only son. All the popular families have always created alliances through marriage. We can't just marry because we found a decent girl Ed. That decent girl needs to come from a decent family."

"Where did you find her?" Smith asked.

"At Frank Steward's party," I replied.

"How? How was she invited?" Frank asked.

"She is friends with Michelle Hutchinson," I replied.

Another round of silence came at the table. Kane and Smith kept exchanging glances. I had a sense of what was at the tip of their tongue. It was the same reason I had kept away from Sarah after that unforgettable night.

"I hope you didn't raise her hopes up. I hope you made her understand that you can't be with her?" Kane asked.

I was quiet and unresponsive. I picked up the bottle of wine and refilled my glass.

"God. Don't do this Ed. It's not going to be a good business decision," Smith added.

"Why does it have to be a business decision? I found a gorgeous woman. She is intelligent. She has a great fashion sense. She is soft-spoken. Those are the things that should matter," I added.

"Now you sound like a child," Smith said, shaking his head.

"Deep in your mind you know the truth Ed. You know your parents will not consent to this. I know you're doing alright on your own, but marriage to the wrong lady would send the wrong message to your competitors and allies," Kane added.

"She is not the wrong girl," I insisted, taking a gulp of wine. "She is the one I have fallen in love with."

Kane shook his head, took another deep breath and reclined in the chair. He was slightly frustrated with me.

"You have to really think about this Ed. You don't want to make the wrong move at this stage of your life. You have a small family. You don't want to make it smaller," Smith advised.

I took a sip of wine and sat back. I understood their concerns, and to be fair, I had taken my time to consider Sarah's suitability after my research on her.

Nonetheless, Sarah felt right, and I was slightly afraid that I was taking too much time to start a journey that would bring me so much happiness.

VIII

SARAH

Saturday evening was boring for me. I had spent most of the morning working on my novel, but I was still shackled by a lack of interest in other things.

I couldn't bring myself to watch a movie, and I wasn't really hungry after drinking coffee in the morning.

My sense of loneliness became emboldened, and I found myself asking existential questions. I knew these questions and mood emanated from the frustration and disenchantment that came from not knowing my place in Edmond's life.

It was annoying to be in this situation, to be influenced by an event that lasted no more than two hours. It was annoying that my brief moment with Edmond threatened to define the rest of my life.

Was it because I was an over-thinker? Was it because I was needy?

Perhaps loneliness had a way of impelling the heart to fall for the first person that showed a bit of care. Perhaps I was a victim of my condition. Perhaps I wouldn't have fallen so easily for Edmond if I was extroverted and had plenty friends and companions.

I thought about going outside. Perhaps I could drink a beer or two and feel better. Perhaps I could meet another man that would help demystify and eliminate the condition that kept me unhappy.

I spent time in the bathroom. Afterward, I spent time in the bedroom. I felt lost and confused, walking about aimlessly in my own apartment. It was in the midst of this struggle, I dropped face down on my bed. I didn't know whether to feel sorry for myself or just laugh.

I could go back to working on my novel, but I had a feeling I would struggle. I was more bored than sad.

I spent time in my bed before I returned to the living room. Again, I tried to watch a movie. I resorted to eerie monologues as if I was conversing with someone else in the room.

"This movie is so nice."

"I am sure it'll have a happy ending."

"Well, we'll just have to wait and see."

"What if it doesn't have a happy ending?"

"Happy endings don't really matter. Reality is more vicious."

Although it felt like I was flirting with insanity, I actually felt better and more focused on the movie.

Halfway through the movie, my phone started ringing. It was in my bedroom. I hurried down to the bedroom as if the call was my salvation from the cesspit of boredom.

It was Michelle. Seeing her name on the phone brought a big smile on my face.

"Hello."

"I'm outside your place. Are you home?" Michelle asked.

"Yeah."

"Alright. I'm coming right up."

I punched the air, jubilantly, and screamed at the top of my voice. After screaming, I felt a bit sad that Michelle's call had so much influence on me. I loved her, but I didn't feel so pathetically lonely until I met Edmond at Steward's party.

I waited for Michelle outside my apartment. I had a big smile on my face. Her impending presence already meant so much to me.

Michelle finally showed up with a paper bag containing seven rolls of pancakes and a bottle of wine. I took her to the living room and emptied the pancakes on a flat, ceramic plate.

I brought two glasses, opened the bottle of wine, and filled the glasses halfway.

Michelle and I watched the ongoing movie together. I intimated her on the trajectory of the movie to keep her abreast of the prevailing events and main characters.

We actually enjoyed the movie, and by the time we were done, the wine was already halfway down the bottle.

"I have good news," Michelle said, finally.

"I want to hear it."

"Edmond has broken up with Linda. It happened suddenly. No one really knows what happened between them."

The news made me smile, but it equally made me nervy. If Edmond could lose feelings for Linda without an obvious reason, shouldn't I be worried that I had suffered the same fate?

"You don't look really happy Sarah. Isn't this what you wanted?"

"Yeah, but I haven't heard from him since Friday."

"Seriously?"

"Yeah."

"What do you really mean? He hasn't called? He hasn't asked to see to you? What has he not done?"

"He hasn't done anything. It feels like meeting him at that party was a dream."

"That's strange. He should have called you. He should have said something," Michelle said, ponderously. She dropped her glass on the table.

"Did something happen recently? Something bad perhaps?" I asked.

"I don't think so. This is really strange Sarah. I can't explain it. If I were you, I'd just take my mind off him."

"I have tried."

"What do you mean? You can't take him off your mind? You have only seen him once. Don't tell me you're already so attached."

"I think I am."

"Goddamn it," Michelle bawled, and reclined in her chair.

I took a deep breath and dropped my face. I felt like a fool. I felt like I had been naïve in my dealings with him.

"What really happened, Sarah? What did he tell you? What did he do?"

I inhaled deeply and held forth about my time with him in the party. I took my time, and touched on the small things that defined my romance with Edmond. Surprisingly, talking about this experience brought a bit of joy to my heart.

I looked up at Michelle's face and found a faint smile. She was impressed and touched by the tone that governed my story.

After I finished narrating my experience with Edmond, Michelle became quiet and thoughtful. She looked towards the TV, but I knew she wasn't really watching.

"Do you want me to call him? Maybe I could ask random questions."

"I don't think that is a good idea. I don't want him to think that I have been complaining to you," I replied.

"What are you going to do then?"

"Maybe I should call him. I have his number."

Michelle shook her head, disapprovingly.

"Do you really think you can call him without sounding needy? I don't want you to worsen your situation with him. I don't think this is the right time for you to call him."

"What am I going to do?"

Michelle heaved a heavy sigh and picked up her glass of wine. She took everything in one gulp.

"I know you had a great experience with him. It must have been magical, but maybe his behavior should make you lower your expectation. There is no harm in lowering your expectation, trust me. It makes it easier for you to move on if he cannot replicate the energy he showed you at the party."

"But how do I do that?"

"This is something you have to find on your own. Maybe now is the time to focus on your novel when you're free. Occupy your mind. Time heals all wounds."

"What if he calls? Should I ask him why he hasn't called?"

"If you have to ask him, then he doesn't really care. He has to come clean, Sarah. He has to tell you on his own. I can see you have strong feelings for him, but you can't afford to cheapen yourself."

The silence that followed Michelle's utterance occupied my mind with regret and despair. I was able to put my behavior in the past week in a better perspective.

Although Michelle had alluded to it, I was cheap. I had made myself cheap for him. By thinking about a man that couldn't find the time to keep a simple promise of calling me, I had actually cheapened myself.

"What are you thinking right now?" Michelle asked.

"I don't even know."

"I don't like what I see, Sarah. You're stronger than this. This is why I won't advice anybody to fall in love just like that. It's better to grow in love. It is safer that way. At least you're loving the person because of what they're offering."

I took a deep breath and took the bottle of wine. I filled my glass to the brim and quickly took down the wine in a few gulps.

Michelle had a concerned look, but preferred to remain quiet as she regarded me.

"I'm going to be alright," I said, with a deep exhale.

"Are you sure?"

"Yes."

"Here's what we'll do. If any funny thoughts come to your mind, call me. Do you understand me?"

I nodded.

"I want you to tell me you understand."

"I understand."

Michelle took a quick look at her timepiece and stood up from the chair.

"I have to be on my way now."

I stood up and gave her a warm embrace.

"Thank you for visiting me. I really needed your company."

Michelle stopped in the doorway and turned to me. It was hard to miss the scrims of worry in her eyes.

"Are you really sure you're going to be alright?" Michelle asked.

"I'll be fine."

"You can come with me, you know. My parents traveled to New York this evening. You can spend the night in my room if you feel you won't be comfortable alone."

"That's really thoughtful of you."

"What are friends for?"

"I think I'll be fine. I have to get used to this. Like you said, I have to heal."

Michelle was not impressed, but she embraced me and stroked my hair.

"I will call you tomorrow morning," she said, and walked away.

I remained outside my apartment, slouched against the patch of wall beside the door. The hallway was quiet, but it was noisy inside my head.

After a little while, I mingled with regret. I felt I should have accepted Michelle's offer. Spending the night with her would have offered a better route towards handling my troubles with Edmond.

Back in my apartment, I went to my room and sat down on my bed, reclining against my headboard.

I wasn't sleepy, but I tried not to occupy myself with sad thoughts. I thumbed on my phone and went from one social media app to the other. At this point, nothing offered any real reprieve from the sadness that filled my heart.

Moments later, I received a text from Michelle:

I'm home. Please stay safe and don't think too much about anything.

I smiled, faintly, and dropped my phone on the cabinet beside the bed. The time was just 9:46pm. It was actually too early to sleep on a Saturday, but I felt sleep was the best way to live through these perilous hours. I knew I wouldn't be so sad once I was back to work on Monday.

I struggled to find sleep. If anything, lying down made me susceptible to more thoughts. It felt like several voices in my head were speaking at the same time.

I stood up, suddenly, and picked up my phone. I was afflicted by the sudden urge to reach out to Edmond. I knew I couldn't call him. It would be so difficult to speak to him without breaking down.

I decided to send a text. I typed several texts and kept deleting until I settled for one. It was a short text, but it captured my current situation with him.

After sending the text, I felt slightly peaceful, and the diverse voices in my head fizzled out. I dropped back down in the bed and tried to sleep again.

Sleep continued to elude me, but I wasn't as miserable as I had been before sending the text. Sending the text had effectively softened the pain from Edmond's absence in my life.

IX
EDMOND

Since I was a child, I had always appreciated the way my father looked at my mom. It was the sort of look that sent a clear message of his undying feelings for her.

On their 40th marriage anniversary, my father produced the same expression before my mom. This was a party that happened every year, but that look, that loving look, hadn't changed at all.

This particular party was bigger than the previous anniversary parties. There were more guests, and some of the folks that were single the previous year attended with their wives and spouses. Their progress offered a beautiful spectacle.

Smith and Kane had come with their respective wives, and I had no intention of coming in-between their interactions with their wives. Hence I kept my distance, preferring to stand close to a wall and drinking from a glass of Champagne.

My father loved to organize a party. He would celebrate anything. And he had specially built this hall for his parties. This building sat in a nineteen-acre estate, which was my dad's way of making his own miniature paradise on earth.

Apart from the palatial mansion where he lived, there were several recreational features in the estate. Also, I had a personal duplex home in the estate.

I met Linda at the other side of the wall. It was hard to tell if she could see me from that side, but I could see that she was sitting with her parents.

Linda was different today. Apart from taking a beautiful, demure look, there was no trace of the lady that stuck out her tongue at me at the Blinks Center. She comported herself with high dignity and showcased an innocence that made it difficult to see her dark side.

I had heard whispers from several quarters about my failed relationship with her. There were indications that Linda was unfortunate to be with a man like me.

My father tapped the mic and got the attention of everyone in the hall. He was holding a glass of Champagne, and my mother was holding one as well. They were huddled up together, lovingly.

When my father started speaking, everyone listened. He was full of praises for my mom, who had an arm around his shoulder.

"God has blessed us with a hard-working son, who is doing great on his own. I couldn't have wished for a better son," my father said, scanning the hall. "Where is Edmond?"

Everyone looked over their shoulders in search of me. I knew I couldn't continue to tarry away from the rest of the guests.

I started forward and met my father's eyes.

"There he is," my father said, excitedly. "The man after my own heart."

I received applause from the guests, and I heard inaudible whispers.

Once I climbed up the flight of stairs leading to the overhanging part of the hall, my father gave me a tight embrace. This move increased the sound of applause.

I embraced my mom once I drew apart from him. My mom left a kiss on my cheek.

"Please be happy," she whispered.

I smiled and stood at her side.

"This is not just a celebration of my marriage anniversary. This is a celebration of life. A celebration of the wonderful blessings my family and I have received from life and I thank you all for being a part of it. Enjoy the rest of the party," my father said, and handed the mic to the host.

Two photographers clambered up the stairs and gave us several snapshots. My father took my hand and led me to a corner.

"What's up with you?" he asked.

"I'm fine."

"Are you sure?"

"Yeah."

"You don't look happy, Ed. I don't know what is up with you, but you should know that you have the best support system. Your mom and I want the best for you."

"I know, Dad. I am fine. A man cannot always be over happy. You told me that."

"I know what I told you but today is for celebration. Cast everything away for now. Cheer up."

I nodded and smiled at him.

My father walked towards my mom, who was standing at the top of the stairs. Together, they climbed down the stairs and stopped at the foot of the stairs.

"Come on, Ed. Come join us," my mom said. Reluctantly, I drifted towards them. I preferred to follow the party from a distance, but I didn't want to make any move that would ruin their celebratory mode.

I walked with them to a round table that had an uninterrupted view of the overhung platform. It was just the three of us at the table, but I could see the tables of most of the prominent guests, including the table of Linda and her parents.

Linda was conversational with her father, who was a tiny man with grey hair. Mr. Evans was head of the Thriller fast-food chain, but he was also the owner of the Los Angeles Golden Lions.

"Have a drink, Son," my father said, handing me a glass.

There was food on the table. Chicken and chips, pork, bacon, but I didn't feel like eating anything. I received the drink. It was exactly what I needed.

I took a sip of Champagne and watched as my mom helped a piece of chicken steak in her mouth.

Incidentally, the host introduced a dance group on stage. I watched as the group entertained the guests with several acrobatic moves. They did several break dances. Our guests couldn't stop applauding them.

After the dance group, a musician came on stage. She was a relatively musician but sang Whitney Houston's Greatest Love Of All as if she had been performing all her life. I was impressed.

I was reminded of the lyrics of this song, and I wondered whether I was becoming miserable because I was a victim of the expectations of society. Wouldn't it be great to just live in my own terms?

A comedian came on stage next. He wore a dress and painted his lips. His appearance made the guests laugh even before he said anything.

I turned towards Linda and found that she was still engrossed in a conversation with her father. As I regarded them, Mr. Evans swiveled at me and met my eyes. He had a serious look on his face.

I had a feeling that Linda was intimating him on my decision to break up with her, but I knew she didn't have the mettle to tell the truth.

I turned to my father. He had his eyes peeled on the comedian and chuckled because of something he had said. My mom was also attentive to the comedian, but she wasn't cracked up by his jokes. She had a calm, cheerful look.

Incidentally, my phone beeped as I returned my gaze to Linda and her father. They were still conversational. Mr. Evans had one hand on Linda's shoulder, and Linda loomed her face down.

I took out my phone and met a text from Sarah. Once I saw her name, sticky flushes ran through my stomach.

I took a deep breath and dropped my phone back on the table. I wasn't ready to see her text. I was fraught with guilt and felt I had disappointed myself, ruining chances of creating a true love story with her.

"Is there a problem?" my mom asked.

"I'm fine," I replied.

"You look nervous and you're sweating on your brow."

I took out a hanky from the breast pocket of my suit and wiped my brow. I refilled my glass with Champagne and took a gulp.

I swiveled at Linda's table and met her eyes. She was gawking at me. Mr. Evans was no longer by her side. I took a quick look around the banquet room but didn't find him.

I looked away from Linda, unwilling to be caught up in her nonverbal war.

"You know you can talk to me, right?" my mom asked.

I heaved a heavy sigh, slightly annoyed by her constant show of concern. I settled for a nod and gained a bit of reprieve when she turned back to the comedian.

I picked up my phone and tapped on Sarah's text. It was a short message:

What happened to forever? Is this the point where I give up and accept that everything that happened was a dream?

I took a deep breath and felt an increased surge of guilt inside me. I kept my phone in my pocket, but I became unstable.

I was tormented by the memories of my time with her. I couldn't believe I had waited this long to reach her again. I had no excuse.

I took out my hanky and wiped my brow again. I turned to my mom and met her eyes. Internally, I hoped she wouldn't ask any more question. She didn't. She simply turned back to the comedian.

"I will be right back," I said, taking my drink with me.

My parents simply nodded and turned back to the comedian.

As I walked from the table, I kept my face up to avoid any needless exchange of pleasantries.

I moved to the wall where I had initially observed the party. I took out my phone and reread Sarah's text. I was gripped by the same feeling of guilt and wistfulness.

"Edmond Barker. Look how much you've grown."

I looked up and found Evans in front of me. He had an awkward smile on his face. Immediately I saw him, I had a feeling he was going to talk about my broken relationship with Linda.

"Good evening, Mr. Evans. It's a joy to have you at my parents' party."

"Are you sure?" Evans asked. He had a serious look that unnerved me slightly. Evans looked like a man that had no intention to play nice. I was short of words.

"I got you," he added, chuckling. "Look at your face."

I was relieved to see him chuckling, but I didn't find his question funny. I felt he had spontaneously chosen this move to douse the growing tension between us.

"Everyone seems to be going into real estate investment these days. Maybe I should really consider it," Evans said.

"It is a great place to be in," I replied.

"I am building up more locations for my fast food. I'm already in discussion with your father."

"That's great. I'm happy you're dominating the California fast food market."

"I am proud of you as well, Ed. Your father has told me so many things about you. He says you're a genius."

"Well, my father is great at hyping me up."

"I don't think it's really a hype. Look at what you've done for yourself and yet you're still humble."

"I guess there's so much more to do."

"Some of these things are hereditary, you know. Your father is a great man and now you're great as well."

"Thank you."

"Imagine what we'd become once we unite our families. Linda says you two are having issues, but I hope you guys resolve them soon. There is so much at stake. Generations unborn are counting on the two of you."

Evans's eyes were unblinkingly placed on me. He extended his hand forward and took my hand.

"I've watched you grow, Ed. I know you're a good boy. I know you can control and solve the most difficult problems. I'm counting on you. Don't let us down," he added, loosening his grip on my hand. "I'll see you around," he added, and started towards his table.

I leaned against the wall, putting my hands into my pockets as I kept my eyes on him. Although Evans hadn't made any threat, it felt like I had just received several threats from him. It felt like there would be consequences if I couldn't resolve my problems with Linda.

As I took my hands out my pocket to wipe the sweat that dripped from my brow with my blazer sleeve, I took my phone out. I reread Sarah's message over and over again. I knew I had to see her tonight. Despite my shame and reluctance to message her, the glasses of Champagne took over and I succumbed to the inching desire to see her.

X

SARAH

I was jolted out of sleep by the sound of my phone. I turned away from the cabinet, sleepy-eyed. Although I was awake, I wasn't really conscious of the situation.

My phone stopped ringing and made it easy for me to focus on finding sleep again. Only, it started ringing again and forced me awake. I got up from the bed and picked up my phone.

Sleep instantly left my eyes as soon as I saw Edmond's name. I didn't know whether it made sense to take his call. I stared at the phone screen until it stopped ringing.

Soon after, a text popped up on my phone screen:

Please take my call if you're still awake. If you're asleep, I want you to know I'm sorry. I don't have any excuse for not reaching out since Friday. Although I feel strongly about what I share with you, I'm still healing from my last relationship. I wish I can see you tonight.

I reread his text several times and didn't know how to respond to it. I liked the fact that he didn't try to make excuses, but I wondered if Edmond was stable enough for a relationship with me.

I was fully awake and thought about calling Michelle, but it was already too late.

Incidentally, my phone started to ring again. It was Edmond. I huffed and puffed a few times before I took the call.

"Sarah, Honey. I'm so sorry. I have been foolish. Why have I treated you this way? You are supposed to be my escape. You're supposed to be the one that saves me from the darkness in my life... Are you there?"

I was quiet and gave in to noisy respiration.

"Please say something. Are you there?"

"Yes. Yes, I'm here."

"I know you're mad at me. You deserve to be mad at me. I've messed up."

"You could have just called. You could have just told me about your troubles."

"I was conflicted. Relationship has taught me that business is easier to handle. Nothing has made me feel so foolish."

"What does this mean, Edmond?"

"Don't you want to see me?"

So late in the night?"

"The night is beautiful, Honey."

"Why do you want to see me?"

"To keep to my promises."

"Don't play games with me. You ruined my week."

"I'm sorry. I'm so sorry. But we can do so much tonight. I really want to see you."

"It's going to be difficult. I can't just leave my place and take a cab. I was even already sleeping."

"But you don't have to take a cab. I'm already at your apartment building."

"How? You're kidding."

"I'm not. I may not have reached out to you, but I watched you for some time."

"This sounds creepy."

"I'm sorry."

I was confused and wondered why Edmond preferred to make private research instead of contacting me.

"If you want me to leave, I can leave and come tomorrow morning."

I pondered his statement and felt it offered me an opportunity to set boundaries in my relationship with him.

However, Edmond was not alone in his desire to see me. I felt refreshing flushes in my soul as soon as I heard his voice.

"Just tell me what I should do, Honey."

I stood from the bed and tried to apply the full weight of reason. It was difficult. My heart drummed inside me.

"Let's wait till tomorrow morning," I said, finally.

"Alright then. Good night."

As soon as he hung up, I felt a weakness in my knees. I felt horrible as if I had committed an unforgivable sin.

Unable to stave off this feeling, I thumbed on his number and called him.

"Don't go," I said, as soon as he answered.

"I am still here. I was hoping you'd call back."

Internally, I frowned at his guts. I wasn't sure that I really liked his influence on me. It was particularly frightening that Edmond was aware of his influence on me. In such a short time, he had figured out my expected behavior.

I was uncomfortable, but this feeling of discomfort didn't really matter in the scheme of things. I wanted to see him. I wanted to meet the man that had captured my heart so quickly, and whether I was being manipulated or coopted into his little game didn't really matter.

I felt slightly ashamed as I moved out of my apartment. It felt like I had no choice in offering myself cheaply to him.

In the elevator, I thought about finding a way to minimize Edmond's influence on me. I reckoned it was unhealthy and actually put me in danger of being broken irreparably.

In the elevator lobby, I almost laughed at myself. I couldn't believe I had eased my way into forgiving him. Who was this man that had enchanted me?

Edmond was standing outside his mustang. He wore a grey suit and hurried towards me. I stood at the doorway and watched his approaching frame. How had he managed to maintain the intensity he had showed last Friday without trying to reach out to me in the last seven days?

Edmond clambered up the stairs and embraced me. It was a forceful embrace. If he didn't immediately weave his hands around my back, he would have tipped me over.

Edmond held me tightly as if I was standing at the border of a new country where I had decided to spend the rest of my life away from him.

Although I was happy to see him again, I was shocked and unable to match his intense show of affection.

At one point, he picked me up from the floor and quickly dropped me back down.

"God. I'm crazy. What was I thinking? How could I stay away for so long? I'm not supposed to let the world affect my feelings for you."

Edmond took a step back from me and placed his hands on my cheeks.

"I'm so happy to see you again. I'm so sorry for staying away for so long."

He gave me another warm embrace. I placed my hands on his back this time. I could see that he was truly sorry, but I was afraid. I had a feeling that this could happen again.

"What does this mean? I want to hear it again."

"I want to be with you, Sarah. I really think you're perfect for me."

"Was it because of the text I sent to you? Was that why you decided to come to me?"

"To be fair, it contributed. But I was mostly afraid that I was going to break your heart if I started a relationship with you. There's too much at stake."

"What has changed?" I asked, curiously.

"I don't really care anymore. I just want to fight for what I am about to create with you."

He wrapped his hand around my wrist and curled his other hand around my waist. He drew closer, keeping his face inches away from mine. His lips grazed mine ever so slightly.

My lips trembled. The memory of the last kiss came to the fore of my mind. Slowly, he sucked on my bottoms lip and pulled it slightly before drifting up to my top lip.

Edmond kissed me slowly in the doorway, making the most of the lack of activity in the elevator lobby.

I felt his hands on my buttocks, but as he grabbed them, he pulled his lips away, and stared intently into my eyes.

"Let's go for a ride. The night is clear and beautiful."

Edmond didn't wait for my response before he weaved one hand around my waist and led me away from the elevator lobby.

He led me to his Mustang and opened the door. He waited for me to enter the car and closed the door.

Quickly, he moved to the other side and joined me in the car. Our eyes locked. Brown eyes on sexy grey eyes.

"You are so beautiful," he said, and turned on the ignition.

I was caught up in the mesmerism that gripped me the very first time I met him. Edmond's exhibitions were intense. It felt like a dream.

Perhaps I was still asleep in my apartment. Perhaps this appearance was a product of my vivid imagination.

He took my hand. I wasn't wearing the wristwatch he had gifted me. He took a look at the spot where the wristwatch was supposed to be.

"I didn't remember to wear it," I said.

"It's okay," he said, lifting my wrist to his lips. He kissed it and closed his eyes.

"Is there something you want to tell me?" he asked.

"I don't... I can't even think clearly right now. I didn't expect this."

"What did you expect?"

"I thought this will never happen. I thought you've moved on before we even started."

"I wouldn't blame you for thinking that way. I'm so happy that your feelings for me are still there."

"How am I sure that this is not another round of short-lived pleasure? How am I sure that you won't change after tonight?"

"You will see, Honey. I don't think I'm in the position to feed you with more words. I have said so much already. Now is the time for some action. Actions speak louder."

Edmond's eyes stared pleadingly at me. Although I struggled to understand the sudden change in his behavior, his eyes were tinged with sincerity. I was able to think that he truly loved me from just looking at him. I didn't know how he was able achieve this. I didn't know whether I was simply seeing what I wanted to see.

"I am not sure about this journey, Ed, but I still want to ride with you. I feel I'm crazy for doing this."

"I'm sorry for making this more difficult than it should be. I should have behaved better."

"Please stop apologizing. I understand. You needed to heal. I know how it feels. I am just afraid for what you may do in the future."

Edmond was quiet and thoughtful. He dropped his face and ran his hand across his brow. Something about my words rubbed off on him unpleasantly. It appeared he wasn't sure that he wouldn't hurt me in the future.

His protracted silence started me towards the thought that hurt was a price I would need to pay for becoming entwined with him.

"What? Why are you so quiet?"

"I feel bad that I don't know what the future holds, but we just have to do our best. Maybe my best would be enough."

"It will be enough, alright. But what is really the problem, Ed? What is standing between us?"

"It is mostly my own insecurities."

"I really want this to work. I want to be sure you really want to ride with me."

"Yes. I want to ride with you. I want to ride with you forever."

Edmond looked desperate. He took my hand and left a kiss on my wrist.

"I don't want to lose you. I know we've only just started, but I really believe in my intuition. I have no doubt that you're the one for me."

I couldn't take my eyes from his face. Edmond wasn't as organized as he had been in Steward's party. He was weak and desperate, but I still loved this vulnerable side of him. I loved the fact that he was afraid of losing me.

Perhaps I would always find a way to love every side of him. Perhaps it was what falling in love impelled in my heart. Perhaps I would always find a way to rationalize his behavior and make it appealing to my heart.

"Let's go for the ride," I said, finally.

I looked through the window as he drove down the road. El Sereno was quiet and lonely, like a stranger in a new city. The sparkling edifices that lined the road looked like talented singers without an audience.

Edmond drove slowly and gave me a great opportunity to capture the subtleties of the neighborhood I had lived in since I started working at Hutchinson & Co Legal.

We were uncommunicative until we left the neighborhood. Edmond drove down to Lincoln Heights and drove past my workplace. He stopped outside a club.

It was lively outside the clubhouse, which had an illuminated sign where House 69 was boldly inscribed.

There were a few barely clad ladies at the roadside. Some of them were smoking and looked like hookers. Some sniffed drugs from their hands.

The men were not left out. It was easy to think that the folks that lingered around the club premises were not allowed inside. Perhaps they couldn't afford the entrance fee.

There were a few cheerful folks, who made videos and had fun outside the club.

"Why did you stop here?" I asked.

"I'm not used to being in places like this."

"You have never been in a club?"

"I have, but the clubs I go to are very private. All the faces are familiar."

"Oh. I think I get you. I guess it is one of the privileges of being wealthy."

"Maybe, but I do not really feel free. Sometimes I admire the ordinary guy. Except the ones that do drugs."

"Would you like an experience at an ordinary club?"

"I'm not sure, but I think it would be beautiful. Some of these clubs are decent. They have VIP sections."

"All clubs have VIP sections."

"Everyone is a VIP in the ones I attend."

"Privilege."

"Yeah."

"What do you see, Ed?"

"People. I don't know if they're happy, but if they feel alive, I don't think there's really any privilege."

"Why do you think so?"

"The living feel alive, the dead have no feelings. This defines every one of us."

"It is easier to be philosophical when you don't have to worry about your next meal."

"Do you have to worry about your next meal?"

"No. I guess I'm a bit privileged."

Edmond nodded and sat back in His chair.

"When I was younger, my dad usually took me on random rides around the city. He took me to poor neighborhoods and made sure I understood what was outside my circle."

"Sounds like your dad didn't want you to be caught up in your privilege."

"Yeah. He used to say there are lots of kids that would do great things if they were born in rich families. He said I should never think that I'm better than them."

"Now I'd really like to meet your father."

"He is a great guy. He brought me up in his own way. But it has made it difficult off me to really fit in. Sometimes I want to leave the comfort of my privilege."

"I don't think you should. You could travel, watch movies, there are so many ways to see the other side of the world."

"I think it is more than that. It is so sad that I wouldn't have been in this position if I wasn't born in a wealthy family."

"If I were you, I wouldn't worry myself about that. Inequality has always been a part of the world."

Edmond took a look at me and smiled. He turned to the periphery of the clubhouse and regarded the faces outside.

The barely clad ladies started looking in our direction. Edmond's Mustang easily gave away his financial status. The interests of the ladies settled the doubts I had about them. They were hookers.

One put off her cigarette and drifted towards us.

"This is going to be fun," I whispered.

"Are you looking for some love, tonight?" the lady asked, leaning against the window at my side.

I was sitting back and made it difficult for the lady to capture my presence.

"What love do you have to give?" I asked.

The sound of my voice and its apparent feminine quality put the lady off.

"Oh! My God," she said, and turned away from the car.

Edmond chuckled, becoming livelier as the lady walked away. It was refreshing to see him stave into laughter.

"Do you always stop by the roadside?" I asked.

"This is the longest I've been here."

"I see. One could think you patronize hookers."

"Jesus. Come on."

"What? Did I touch a nerve?"

"No. It's just funny.

"So, it's not something you'd do?"

Edmond regarded me with disbelief.

"I can't believe you're really asking this question."

"Then answer it."

"I don't do that. It's crazy. I don't think I can stoop so low."

Edmond kept shaking his head. He couldn't believe I had actually asked this question. Only, asking this question showed that I had finally gotten used to the fact that Edmond had truly woken me up and taken me for a ride.

"I want you to be with me the next time I'm racing."

"When would that be?"

"It's usually on Fridays. Friday afternoon."

"I'd love to be with you."

Edmond smiled and took my hand. He fixed his fingers in the spaces between my fingers.

"I'm going to make up for lost time," he said.

"I don't want you to stress over what is in the past. I have forgiven you. Just be yourself and try not to hurt me."

He kissed the back of my hand and pulled closer to me. He placed one hand on my cheek and kissed me. It was a short kiss, but he kept stroking my hair after he stopped kissing me.

We began to drive back to my apartment. I was comfortable with him, and I could see he was also comfortable with me. However, I couldn't forget that I had felt this way the first time I met him. Internally, I hoped my relationship with him would follow a normal, predictable route this time.

Edmond parked outside my apartment and gave me kiss on the cheek.

"Do you want to come inside?" I said.

XI

Edmond

Her apartment was cute. Small but cute. Everything was neatly organized and perfectly positioned. I was starting to think she might be more organized than Martha.

She held my hand and guided me towards her couch. As she pulled my arm, she turned back and gave me a cheeky smile.

We sat down onto her sofa and I pulled her legs on top of mine.

"What do you want to watch?" Sarah asked.

"Maybe we could just listen to some music?" I responded.

Sarah decided to play soulful music and commanded Alexa to dim the living room lights. Although it was dark, her eyes still lit up the room.

"You are so beautiful Sarah," I said as I moved my hands from her legs to her face.

Her eyes were fixed on me; they had completely captivated me. I felt like I was under a spell. How had I managed to stay away from her for this long?

She leaned in and kissed me. Her lips felt 100 time softer than they did when we were in the car.

She drew me in closer and wrapped her arms around my neck. My heart began to race 200 miles an hour. I was scared that this would give away how much I was truly in love with her.

I could feel my penis beginning to rise, but luckily my bottoms were able to somewhat hide what was going on below.

Sarah moved from besides me and sat on top of my lap whilst still kissing me intensely and passionately.

XII

Sarah

As I sat on his lap, I could feel his hard penis pushing against my leg. If only Ed knew I was already dripping, and my panties were wet. This was somewhat embarrassing. How was he able to turn me on so much just from kissing? Was this due to the lack of sex in my life?

It was at this point that Edmond lifted me up into the air and I wrapped my legs around him. I didn't realize how strong he was and I didn't think it was possible for him to be any sexier in my eyes.

"Where is your bedroom?" he asked. His greys eyes were filled with passion and his lips were wet from kissing me.

"That door over there," I said, pointing towards my bedroom.

He walked towards the door, still carrying me, and swung the door open.

Edmond threw me onto the bed and ripped off his shirt. His body was to die for.

He slowly crawled onto the bed, and I lifted up my arms so that he could help me to take off my night dress. Edmond slowly kissed my neck as he used his hands to take off my bra.

My breast bounced down as they were freed from the chains off my underwear.

I laid with my back faced down on the bed. Edmond passionately kissed my lips before he made his way down, kissing every part of my body on the way. He started on my neck as he sucked and bit me passionately. When he got to my breast, he supped on them succulently like a baby longing for his mother. He did something so interesting with his tongue that I couldn't help myself but to moan.

He continued down my body, kissing my stomach before he got to my vagina. He used his teeth to pull down my panties and came back up, inserting his tongue deep inside my clitoris. Edmond's tongue was magical. I was oozing out cum at this point and my body vibrated with every move that he made. I wanted more. I needed more.

Edmond came back up and returned to kissing my lips. The body heat between us was immense and I could feel the sweat from our bodies pooling together.

His pants were still on at this point, and I wanted them off so badly. I could already tell from the bulge pressing on my leg that he was huge.

He stopped kissing me for a second and looked deep into my eyes.

"I want you so bad Sarah Barry," Edmond said as he stroked the top of my head, "but I'm trying to be respectful."

Ugh. Respectful. I couldn't even be angry at him for trying to be a gentleman but all I wanted was him inside of me.

"Mmhmm," I responded. I didn't know what else to say.

"I see a future with you Sarah. I don't want to rush things with you. I want everything to be perfect."

Ed was perfect to me. The way he spoke to me. The way he made me feel.

"I completely understand Ed."

He let out a deep sigh and rolled off from on top of me. He began to stare at the ceiling for a couple of minutes before he turned towards me and kissed me on my cheek.

I couldn't help but to smile. Ed honestly made me so happy.

He spooned me and I fell asleep wrapped in his arms.

XIII

SARAH

It was in the Blinks Center I had a vivid sense of some of the privileges of the wealthy folks in Los Angeles.

Edmond had a special card that gave him access to the center and its facilities. The center was only open to its members and their guests.

Edmond chose a white Mercedes for this ride. There was a large swimming pool along the road with an artificial shower. A handful of ladies on bikinis sipped away on margaritas and held up their iPhones.

It was a slow ride, which I perceived was a deliberate move by Edmond to give me a clear view of the center. There was a building beside the sophisticated pool, which looked a bar and lounge.

I met a white building at the other side of the road. It was a library, which came as a surprise to me. I didn't think a place like this would have a library.

There were lots of activities in other buildings by the roadside, but there was a shortage of participants. It was like going to the Santa Monica Pier and meeting only five children.

Moments later, Edmond drove down to a network of roads that served as a racing track. He pulled up around several exotic cars. The drivers sat on the bonnets of their cars, conversational and exuberant.

There were more people at this side of the center.

Four ladies held up a glass box filled to the brim with dollars. They danced, bizarrely, with the box. The ladies looked like professional strippers, but they were not the only one's dancing.

The spectators participated. Some had large bottles of wine in their hands. Some men snuffed cocaine from the cleavages of other women.

It was at this point I realized that equating wealth with sanity had been a misconception. Whether the half-naked ladies were hired to serve the needs of these men was a question I couldn't ask.

Edmond was already in a conversation with two friends. He took my hand, but I was drawn to the activities around me. The folks around the road looked like they could have unprotected sex at the roadside. It certainly looked like something they had tried before.

Apart from the exotic cars on the road, there were other exotic cars at the sides of the road. Hence the spectators weren't just ordinary people at the roadside.

Some sat on top of their cars. Some cars danced, moving up and down to the sound of music. It felt like I had been transported to a modern representation of Sodom and Gomorrah.

"She is the one," Edmond said, stroking my hair. Edmond's friends were not excited to see me. They simply smiled and extended their hands towards me.

"These are my closest friends, Smith and Kane."

"Welcome," Kane said.

"Thank you."

"You really are beautiful," Smith added.

"Thank you."

"All the best," Kane said, moving to his car.

"See you," Smith said, giving Edmond a bizarre handshake, before moving to his car.

"The race starts in five minutes," Edmond said, weaving his arm around my shoulder.

"It doesn't look safe. You would race with people that are half-drunk?" I asked.

"Half-drunk? Come on. The racers don't drink until the end of the race."

"Are you sure?"

Edmond weaved his hands around my waist and pulled me closer. He pressed his forehead against mine.

"I have been doing this for a long time, Honey. I'm really hoping you'll bring me some luck."

"I don't like the sound of that. Don't make it about me. If you're a lousy driver, you'll lose," I said, giving him a painless nudge. Edmond chuckled and left a kiss on my forehead.

A red Ferrari pulled up at the other side of the road. It made an awkward turn that caught my attention.

A beautiful lady on sunglasses climbed down from the car. She had brown hair that wobbled ever so slightly as she drifted towards the road.

She held a bottle of water and took a gulp as she reached the road.

I turned to Edmond and noticed that he was also looking at the lady. He turned towards me, quickly, and took a deep breath. Edmond suddenly looked nervous. He left a kiss on my forehead.

"I'll see you after the race," he said, leaving a kiss on my cheek.

"Don't drive recklessly," I said, turning away from him.

As I walked away from the road, I realized that the brown-haired lady had taken off her sunglasses. She had a glare in her eyes as she kept them on me.

It was at this point I had a sense of her identity. She had to be Linda Evans.

Linda threw away the bottle of water, ensuring that I noticed that she was pissed off. Her behavior made me uncomfortable. I took my eyes away from her, but I knew she was still looking in my direction.

Internally, I hoped she wouldn't stave into a hostile confrontation about my relationship with Edmond. I looked towards the other side of the road where most of the drunk, uncontrolled spectators were situated.

I wished I had chosen that side. There were more people at that side of the road, and it was easy to think Linda would be easily stopped if she tried to do anything stupid.

I glanced at Linda, met her frowned face, and gravitated towards the other spectators at my side of the road.

Moments later, I was standing five yards away the cheerleaders. The sound of gunshot rent the air. It was the signal to start the race, but it made it nervous.

My heart drummed severely, and I clutched my chest, looking left and right. I was afraid that Linda might have pulled out a gun and shot at me.

Linda had a smile on her face. It was an ambiguous smile. She walked towards me, taking her attention from the race. And she intended to make sure that I knew she was looking at me.

I dropped my face, caught up in the voices in my head. I turned to the cheerleaders, who, surprisingly showed no interest in the race. They preferred to dance with the box of cash and make soft, sexy giggles.

I turned to the other side of the road and discovered that a few of the spectators were not focused on the race. It seemed the dancing, cocaine-sniffing, and drinking was a different sport subsumed in the racing contest.

"So, it is you," Linda said, in a soft, whispering voice.

I pretended not to hear her. I took a few steps to the other side and walked past the cheerleaders.

I looked over my shoulder. Linda hadn't followed me, but my movement had attracted the eyes of the people at the roadside. It seemed I wasn't supposed to walk past the cheerleaders.

Two cheerleaders conversed in hushed tone and kept their eyes on me. Embarrassed, I dipped my hand in my bag and took out my phone. I pressed the phone against my ear, pretending to make a call.

I was embarrassed as I placed the phone against my ear. I loomed my face down and moved past the cheerleaders, returning to the position I had occupied beside Linda.

I was speaking on the phone, pandering to a script that was designed to minimize my sense of embarrassment. I backed away from the road and towards a tall building that overlooked it.

Moments later, I dropped the phone back in my bag and looked forward. Apart from Linda, no one else was looking in my direction.

I fixed my eyes on her, steeling myself. It became clear that Linda was set out to embarrass me, and I knew that giving off a timid vibe would only strengthen her.

We locked eyes for a while. She had small, brown eyes and the smile on her face started to broaden. She started towards me, sashaying, and seemingly confident.

I was shaken by her confidence. I didn't think I was in my comfort zone. I didn't think I was in a position to give her as much as she intended to give me.

I thought about backing all the way to the building behind me, but I knew it wouldn't save me from her. Linda looked like a woman that was used to getting what she wanted.

Instead, I stood my ground and tried to look strong.

"What are you afraid of, Bastard?" Linda asked.

"I see you have no manners. I don't want any problem."

"You made that decision when you started following Edmond. He belongs to me."

"He is not a property."

"Yes. He is. He's my property and you're trespassing."

"If he is really your property, why don't you ask him yourself? Why isn't he with you?"

"I see you have a big mouth, Girl. But trust me, you don't want to mess with me. I wish you had asked around before making the decision to date him. There is a reason you met him single. He belongs to me," Linda said, tapping her cleavage.

"I have heard about you. You're the ex."

Linda chuckled and bit on her bottom lip. She was biting hard and frowning her face. I took a step back as her right hand convulsed to a fist. It looked like she intended to resort to thrusts and blows.

"You are too small for me, Girl. Can't you see? You're going to regret this. I am just giving you a heads up. This is my way of caring for you, Girl. Once I start shooting, I don't stop."

"Why do you think you're the only one that can shoot?"

My question unnerved her slightly and sliced off a bit of the confident look in her eyes. She took a deep breath and loosened her right fist.

I hadn't ever been involved in a physical battle, but Linda didn't know that. It was easy to think that my question and look gave her the impression that I was used to fighting dirty.

"I am going to take Ed back, but I'm not going to spare you even after I've had him. I'll still come for you and make sure you're on your knees."

Linda's tone was frightening and sent cold flushes through my stomach. Thankfully, it was the end of the threat.

The sound of cheers got the attention of Linda. The racers were in the last lap. Linda started towards the road and joined in the cheering.

She suddenly didn't look like the woman that intended to embarrass and belittle me. This part of her was likable, and if she had only shown this part, I would have been worried that her breakup from Edmond was caused by his shortcomings.

Although Linda's threat sounded serious, this cheering side of her was more threatening. She looked like the kind of lady that could destroy another person and successfully make herself the victim.

Linda squatted and tapped the interlocked floor. She had a big smile on her face.

She was able to suck out my joy and make me apprehensive with this move. Somehow, I had a strong feeling that I was in trouble. She had the money to sponsor any form of calumny against me.

I started to flirt with the thought of apologizing to her and starting off on a better ground, but I was sane enough to realize that it wouldn't make my situation better.

The sound of screaming and cheering intensified. Edmond's car was ahead of the pile. I hurried towards the road, edging ahead of Linda.

After Edmond crossed the finishing line, I ran towards his car. I ran through the sidewalk, determined to be the first person to congratulate him.

Edmond was already out of his car before I got to him, he stretched out his arms and curled them around my back as I ran into him.

Edmond picked me from the road and made several turns. He kissed my forehead before dropping me back on the road.

"You're my good luck charm," he said, leaving a kiss on my cheek.

Edmond had his hand around my shoulder as we walked towards the cheerleaders who danced and swarmed around him.

Two photographers came along and took snapshots of Edmond and the cheerleaders.

"Come on," Edmond said, beckoning me to join him.

His call made me emotional. I could see he wanted me to be a part of everything.

Edmond took pictures with the drivers, but he also made sure I was part of it. Kane and Smith stuck around him and made light jokes about the race.

I looked around the road but couldn't find Linda. I found her Ferrari, which indicated that she was still around.

As we made our way down to the building that overlooked the road, Edmond handed the box of cash to me.

There was a lot of money in that box. It looked like I would need to work for almost two years to earn what was inside.

In any case, I kept looking over my shoulder. I believed that Linda would suddenly pop up and display a bit of madness before me.

"Are you looking for someone?" Edmond asked, placing his hand on my waist.

"No," I said, feigning a smile.

I remained careful and observant, detached from the ongoing conversation between Edmond and his friends.

In the building, Edmond took my hand and left a kiss at the back of my hand.

"I knew you'd bring me good luck," he said.

"I think you are just a great driver."

"But I haven't been winning for some time. You made that happen."

Kane and Smith clambered up the stairs at the side to the top floor. There was a bar at the ground floor, but there were several doors scattered around the floor, which gave me the impression that several guests rooms were squeezed into the building.

Edmond took me to the top floor, using his fingerprint to gain access to the floor. The floor was warmer, and tufts of smoke swirled languidly around the floor.

There were several tables on one side where masseurs attended to the guests, half-naked with towels draped over their waist down to their knees. Some of the masseurs were women, and some of the guests looked like they had already fallen asleep.

"This looks nice," I said, impressed.

"The female massage section is through that door," Edmond said, pointing to a door at the side.

"Great."

"Don't you want a massage?"

"No. I didn't have it in mind."

"Well, I'll have to freshen up."

"That's okay."

"Want to come with me?"

"There would be other men there, right?"

"It's the men's bathroom."

"I'll just wait in the bar."

"You don't have to go downstairs. Just wait in the lounge," Edmond said, pointing to another door.

"Alright."

He gave me a kiss on my forehead before proceeding through the door that led to the men's bathroom.

With the glass box containing his prize money in my hands, I moved towards the door leading to the lounge. I opened the door and found Linda in the doorway.

It appeared she was about to open the door before I did. Her presence sent grim flushes up my spine.

"The bitch that's going to lose at the end," she said, nudging me away from her path.

I was surprised by the force of her nudge. It was a painful nudge. I stood in the doorway, rubbing the point of impact.

Surprisingly, Linda stopped at the door leading to the men's bathroom. She turned towards me and smiled. She raised two fingers up and pointed them at me before she walked through the door.

I pondered Linda's bizarre move as I moved to the lounge. The lounge was air-conditioned and cool.

I sat down on a couch and examined the glass box. I thought the prize money was incredible for such a short, pleasurable race, but I understood the situation.

There was a concrete cubicle at the top of the lounge. There was a lady in the cubicle and there were several bottles of drinks hanging in the refrigerated shelf etched on the wall.

I kept thinking about Linda's suspicious move and the motive behind it. Although I tried to keep my mind away from it, I couldn't help my increased sense of paranoia. It was hard to dismiss the feeling that Linda had gone for Edmond.

As I sat back on the couch, I thought about heading to the men's bathroom. I stood up from the couch and dropped back down.

It was easy to think there would be lots of bathrooms down there. How could I determine the bathroom of Edmond? Would I just walk down the hallway and scream his name? And if I did that, what would Edmond think of me?

I didn't think it made sense to fight for my relationship with Edmond by using Linda's tactics. I was afraid I could end up becoming like her.

Also, I wasn't familiar with the laws that governed this center. Perhaps there was a big fine and punishment for going to the men's bathroom alone.

I looked towards the bartender and met her eyes. I had a feeling she was waiting for me to call for her attention.

I held up Edmond's prize money, reminding myself that he had handed it to me. He had trusted me with it. I was the one he chose for the snapshots after winning. I was the one he kissed and called his good luck charm. I was the one he wanted to be in the bathroom with.

I initiated a thought process that clarified my relevance in his life. Although I became strengthened and relaxed, there was still a bit of fear inside me. Linda looked like a really determined woman. She looked like she knew how to make everything work together for her good.

XIV

EDMOND

Soaked in warm water, eyes closed, the memory of the race was vivid in my mind. Victory brought a refreshing feeling. It was great to win before Sarah.

Her presence might have no real bearing on my performance, but I saw changes. The way I felt, the way I embraced the world around me, and the way I was focused.

From the first day I met Sarah, I had believed she was going to be a compensation for the heartbreaks and disappointments, and this feeling had grown stronger and stronger every day.

The water dropped noisily on the bathroom floor. I felt warm and wished Sarah was standing before me.

I tilted my face up to face the shower as warm water splashed against my face, and then something incredible happened.

I felt a hand on my shoulder. The hand was soft, and softly moved to my chest. Fingers stroked my nipple. I thought it was Sarah. I thought she had decided to surprise me until I opened my eyes.

"Linda."

"Yes, Honey."

"No. I'm not your honey," I barked, searching for my towel.

It was already with her. My towel was hanging down from her shoulder. She looked at my penis and smiled.

"I have missed this."

"Don't start. Please."

"Start what? You know you love me. You know you love what I have down here," she said, tapping her crotch. "Isn't that why you call me juicy? You like it. And you always liked when I'm in charge."

I backed away from her, but she kept coming. Linda was prepared. She had taken off her dress and left her perky breasts bare. She wore white G-string panties and took a seductive look at me.

I reached for the shower valve, willed to turn it off, but Linda grabbed my hand and tucked herself between me and the valve. I didn't want to be rough with her because I knew she would find a way to use it against me.

She dropped her eyes on my penis and smiled, running her tongue around her top lip.

"I am going to make it grow hard. You know I always make you really hard."

"Why are you doing this?"

"Shh," Linda responded, placing her forefinger on her lips. "Let's enjoy the moment."

"I'm not doing anything with you."

"Are you sure? Little Dicky doesn't think the same way as you. Little Dicky wants me."

Unfortunately, my penis was half-erect, but it was simply an innocuous response to what was before me.

Linda dragged her panties down from her waist slightly.

"I know you more than anyone. You're my baby. Remember how I always pet you? How you call me Mommy? Mommy is back."

"No. I have moved on. I have found someone else."

"That's okay. You can always leave her. We are meant for each other."

"We are not meant for each other. I caught you cheating, Linda. You cheated on me. If you respected me, you wouldn't have cheated. The only reason I've kept quiet about this is because I don't want to ruin your name."

Linda was unmoved by my words. She dragged her panties down from her waist.

"No. No. I made a mistake, but it only make us stronger. The only reason you haven't said anything is because you know I'm going to be the mother of your children. You know we are meant to be together."

Linda grabbed her breasts with both hands and shook them ever so slightly.

"You want mommy to feed you, don't you? Just say yes. Come on, Baby. Say yes."

I took a deep breath, gripped by the memories of my previous sexual experiences with her.

My penis grew and the smile on Linda's face grew wider and wilder.

"That's my baby. That's my beautiful, responsive baby," Linda said, pressing her body against mine. Linda smelt amazing. Her perfume alone was enough to draw kings onto her and I had forgotten how good her breast felt rubbed against my body. I could feel her hard nipples stabbing my chest.

I was powerless and weak before her. I fought all temptation in the world to keep my hands to myself.

"You're mine today, tomorrow, and always," she whispered in my ear, as she nibbled on the bottom of my ear lobe.

I held her face and looked into her eyes, but at the moment the memory of being with Sarah outside House 69 came to mind. The promises I had made to Sarah echoed in my mind.

I slowly drew apart from Linda and picked my towel from her shoulder. She grabbed my hand, pressing her long fingers into my wrist.

"Don't walk away from me. I'm the one for you."

This was a different Linda. She had lost the audacity that brought her to my bathroom. She was swimming towards misery and regarded me, pleadingly.

"You have to move on, Linda. We don't have a future together."

"No. You don't know what you're saying. You're just mad at me. I'm sorry. I'm so sorry. We have been dating for four years. Don't forget that. Please don't forget that."

"It was not important to you, Linda. If I didn't catch you cheating, you'd have continued to pretend that you love me so much."

"I love you so much. It was just a mistake."

I drew my hand apart from hers, but Linda dropped down on her knees and grabbed my leg.

"You are embarrassing yourself."

"No. No. I want you. I want you so much."

I pulled my leg away from her grip and moved out of the bathroom. Linda bawled, screaming at the top of her voice.

I could see her dress in the walled clothesline in the small room leading to the bathroom and toilet.

I wiped my body and quickly put on my underwear. As I tried to wear my pants, Linda came out of the bathroom. She had a glare in her eyes.

"This is not over. You'll come to your senses. You'll realize that I'm the one for you. And I'll keep fighting for you."

She looked crazy and terrible, and if anything, I pitied her. I could see that she hadn't been able to make herself believe that I could move on from her.

XV
EDMOND

I met my father in my duplex home. He had made himself comfortable. He was drinking from a glass of wine and watching TV. It was National Geographic Wild.

He sat up as soon as he saw me and tapped the space beside him.

"Come sit down, Son."

I was slightly apprehensive. This was an unprecedented move. I was slightly helped by his calm, cheerful look.

He fixed his eyes on the glass box containing my prize money for a moment.

"You have been having fun," he said.

"I won this from racing at Blinks."

"You won it from gambling."

"Not really."

"It is gamble, Son. But it's alright. At least you're not an addict."

"Is there a problem, Father?"

"Problem? No. If there was a problem, I'd have called you."

"I can't remember you ever waiting for me here."

"Maybe I just wanted to see how you're getting along."

"But that's not it, is it?"

"You are a man now. You're thirty. Three decades on this earth…and yet the world hasn't really changed. You look at the TV, the lion and its pride need food. The hyenas need food. The leopards need food. The antelopes, the deer, everyone needs food. And yet some of them would lose their lives to feed the others."

"What point are you trying to make?" I asked.

"Have you ever wondered what would happen if all the lions become vegetarians?"

"They would start eating vegetables, I guess."

"Now imagine if there's just one remaining lion that is not a vegetarian. How long would it survive?"

"I don't know."

"He is going to die soon. He will try to hunt. Maybe a buffalo. Once there's an ambush, no other lion would try to rescue him. That's the problem of being alone in issues where uniformity matters."

"I'm still waiting for the point you're trying to make, Father."

"As a young man, I became philosophical. My father taught me a lot. He said I needed other eyes to see the world for what it is. And that's what I've tried to do with you. What are you, Son? Are you among the lions that became vegetarians, or are you the one lion that continues to eat meat?"

I took a deep breath and dwelt on his question. My father was quiet. He sipped from his glass and looked at the TV. He was focused on the TV and didn't have the look of a man that had just asked a question.

"That one lion can still hunt successfully, grow old, and die."

"That's a possibility, but it is said that wise people strengthen their possibilities. Wise people find a middle point between emotion and reason."

"You think I'm too emotional, Father?"

"You are Edmond. Whatever you feel, that's what you are. Are you going to survive in the new world?"

"You don't think I'll survive?"

"This is not about me, Son. This is about you. This is about the decisions you take every day. They would define you. They will make you. They'll break you."

"Why did you want to have this discussion with me?"

"You are my son. Do I need another reason?"

"You trust in me, Father. You trust in my wisdom."

"I do, but I wonder if you trust in yourself. I wonder if you understand the decisions you are making."

"Did Mr. Evans talk about me and Linda?"

"That is usually the only thing he talks about when we talk. He admires you, Ed. He has big plans for the future."

"Now I get where the Lion parable comes from."

"Don't be narrow, Son. It covers everything you can think of. I want you to set a mark and follow it."

"That is what I've always done."

"You told me about Linda two years ago. You said she was perfect for you. You were invited to several dinners with her family…"

"I was wrong about her."

"No. You were naïve. A man would not be strong in every aspect of his life, but he must choose his enemies carefully."

"I don't have anything against her family."

"Linda is part of her family. And your problem with her seems to have created a bit of a situation."

"A situation?"

"This is the fourth time in a week that Evans has called for me to talk to you. If you leave Linda, her family will see it as a betrayal."

"This is crazy."

"In fact as I speak to you, Steward, Hutchinson, and Evans are in communication. We may be looking at the biggest merger we've seen in the real estate industry."

"They still won't be bigger than us."

"Everything takes time, Ed. You have to look in the mirror and do more introspections. In this world, it is difficult to survive as the lion that eats meat."

"She cheated on me."

"That's sad, but you chose her. What if you were already married to her? Divorce would be next, wouldn't it?"

"Of course."

"Linda is an only daughter. You're an only son. The alliance between you two would be one of the biggest in the US."

"What about love, Father? What if I've loved someone else?"

"I'm not going to make a decision for you. That's not why I've come here," my father said, taking a gulp of wine. "I have come to expose the possibility curves to you. You have to know what you're up against. It's like what you see in the animal kingdom. Sometimes you eat because you don't want to get eaten."

My father stood up from the chair, dropped the glass on the stool at the side, and stretched. His body made snapping sounds.

"I haven't had a good sleep this week. Hopefully, I will sleep well tonight," he added, and made a deep exhalation. He walked towards the exit and stopped at the door.

"You don't have to think about it tonight. Sleep on it. Make a wise decision," he added, and walked through the door.

XVI
SARAH

It was after I alighted from Edmond's Mercedes that I realized that I was staring at the biggest party that I had attended in my life.

We were in Hollywood. I saw a Helicopter land on a helipad at the roof of a building beside the Benny Center. The Benny Center was one of the largest event centers in California, and today was the birthday of the owner, who was also the owner of the biggest publishing firm in the US.

The cars in the parking lot were expensive, luxurious cars. There were brand of cars that I hadn't seen on the road. Like Edmond's Mercedes, most of the cars were customized to match the personal preferences of the owners.

I wore a long, blue dress and black shoes. Edmond expressed a romantic chivalry in helping me carry my black bag. He wore a black suit and his shoes, which were black, looked easily expensive.

There were throngs of security personnel outside the center. Chips looped down from their ears, and they moved about, passing relevant information.

As we made our way from the parking lot, a steward came to us. He bowed.

"I'll show you to your table, Mr. Barker, Miss Barry," he said, and edged ahead of us.

There were lots of stewards, and it was easy to see that every table in the center had at least a steward assigned to it.

The entrance door to the center was large and monstrous. It was more than twelve feet in height and width.

An orchestra was already performing as we walked into the center and followed the steward to our table.

It was a large round table, and we were not going to be alone at the table. Twelve chairs were adjoined to the table.

There were already several bottles of wine and champagne on the table.

"Would you like a drink right away?" the steward asked. Edmond and I exchanged quick glances.

"Yeah. Wine please," Edmond said.

The steward stepped forward and uncorked a bottle of wine. He took out the covers pinned on two glasses and filled them halfway. Afterward, he moved behind us.

The tables in the center were spaced out neatly. Our table was stationed in a great position that allowed us a clear view of the top of the center.

The rendition of the orchestra was glorious. It was in Latin, but it was still beautiful even though I didn't know the lyrics. I received goosebumps from the melody. And for a moment, I thought about my life.

It had been a rollercoaster, but there was no doubt that I had continuously made progress. Fate had randomly gotten me attached to the right people. I turned to Edmond and found him staring at my hair.

"What?" I asked.

"You are so beautiful tonight," he said. He leaned forward and left a kiss on my cheek. "I'll kiss you every day. Your face is to die for."

The tone of Edmond's voice conspired with the melody from the orchestra to drain me in a mesmerism that I couldn't resist.

My eyes were suddenly wet and the rash of gooseflesh on my arms became emboldened. I couldn't control the surge of emotion that tarried inside me.

Tears gathered my eyes, and because I couldn't wrap my mind around the source of the tears, I didn't know how to stop them. It felt like an impalpable force suddenly took charge of my body.

I took my bag from Edmond's thigh and unwittingly gave him a clear view of the trickles of tears in my eyes.

I took out a handkerchief from my bag and wiped my eyes, but I was still very emotional. Was it the music? Was it the realization that I had always found a way to make progress in my life?

"Is there a problem?" Edmond asked. I feigned a smile. It was the hardest I had tried, but this feeling and its accompanying explicit emotions persisted.

"Are you alright?" Edmond asked, drawing closer.

"Yes. Yes. I'm fine."

My voice didn't come out right. It betrayed my attempt to downplay my current state of mind.

"You are not fine," Edmond said, seriously.

I turned to him after drying out the tears in my eyes. He was concerned and interested, but I didn't know what to say to him. I didn't know how to make him believe that the tears had simply come on their own without any discernable feeling. It wasn't normal for a person to just cry, but I was crying and the melody from the orchestra was growing thinner and more beautiful.

"Talk to me, Honey. What happened?"

"It is the music. It's so beautiful."

Edmond became quiet and puzzled. He glimpsed at the orchestra and swiveled back at me. His eyes were constricted and his head was slightly cocked. He listened to the orchestra as if he could understand the emotions that gripped me if he listened long enough.

"What is in the music?" he asked.

"I don't know. It's... I guess it just makes me emotional."

"That's a bit strange. Maybe the song touched a part of you that you're trying to hide."

I shook my head, unwilling to accept this notion. I reached for my glass and took a gulp of wine. The wine made me feel better.

"It is okay. I'm better now."

Edmond was not satisfied with the way I had resolved this situation. Clearly, he wanted more explanation, but sadly, I wasn't in the position to grant it. If it was any consolation, I sought for answers internally. I relied on a hearted introspection that momentarily dragged me into my mind.

It was the applause that followed the end of the performance that jolted me off my reverie. Incidentally, Edmond was exchanging pleasantries with some of the arriving guests that were designated to share the table with us.

These guests were brought in by their own stewards, and as we shared pleasantries, Linda and her parents came to the table. It was a crazy turn of event that made me anxious.

Linda wore a sparkling red dress, and actually smiled at me, like a well-wisher, cheering my romance with Edmond.

I drew closer to Edmond and watched as he exchanged pleasantries with Linda's parents. They had a solemn, stern look.

"Meet Sarah," Edmond said, weaving his arm around my shoulder.

Sarah's parents were not interested in my introduction and made it clear before me as they went to their respective seats.

I looked up at Linda and met that devilish sweet smile on her face. She took the seat next to Edmond. Linda's parents sat next to her.

I picked up my glass of wine and took another gulp. I was nervous but tried to steel myself. I knew I wouldn't have attended the party if I knew that Linda and her parents would be sharing the table with us.

"Are you alright?" Edmond asked, whispering.

"Yeah. I'm fine."

Edmond placed one hand on my shoulder, endearing himself to me. I took a glance at Mr. Evans and found a glare in his eyes before he quickly smiled as soon as he saw that I was looking back at him.

The orchestra started singing again, sifting out a compelling melody that left most of the guests entranced. It was quiet in the center. It appeared that most of the guests were used to listening to this sort of rendition.

The performance at the top of the center was projected at the various corners of the center to prevent the guests from straining their necks to effectively capture the performance.

For the most part, the performance served as a distraction for me. I could afford to look away from the guests at the table and pretend that I wasn't huddled up with Linda and her parents.

Unfortunately, this performance was shorter than the first one. And as the guests applauded, I met the searching eyes of Mr. Evans. He had a terrible, intimidating look.

"Did you know they'd be sitting with us?" I asked, whispering to Edmond.

"Who?"

"I know Linda. I know what she was to you. She confronted me at Blinks."

"Why didn't you tell me?"

"I didn't think it was serious. She sounded like an entitled ex."

"That's what she is."

"Are you sure you are telling me everything? Why is she so confident that she can take you back?"

"Don't mind her. She has always been that way."

"Do you work for the Barker Estates, Miss Sarah Barry?" Mr. Evans asked. I was shocked to hear his voice. It was husky and deep, like the voice of a damned smoker.

Also, I was particularly concerned that he knew my full name without knowing where I worked.

"No. She is a devoted legal practitioner," Edmond answered.

"Practitioner? That's interesting."

"She is a paralegal at Hutchinson Legal," Linda cut in.

"A supervising paralegal," Edmond cut in.

"It's a loose way to say she is one of the oldest serving paralegal in the firm," Linda chipped in.

"Miss Sarah has given me peace since she came into my life. She has been the required sunshine in my life," Edmond added.

Linda became quiet, but she didn't lose the smile on her face. She took a glass of wine and raised it to her face.

I appreciated the silence that came from Edmond's remark, and although I would have preferred to answer for myself, I didn't think that Edmond did a particularly bad job.

The host at the top of the center was making a light joke about Mr. Benny and how he had managed to create a monopoly like a God.

The remaining guests assigned to our table finally arrived. They were friendly and cheerful, and resorted to embraces and sincere exchanges.

I was particularly impressed by a sinewy, blonde-haired, winsome man. He wore a resplendent blue suit and shook Edmond's hand before pulling him.

"It has been a while, Ed," the blonde-haired man said.

"Have you been in the country?" Edmond asked.

"Not really. I have been in France for the last two months," he said, turning towards me.

"Who is this beautiful lady?" he asked.

"She is my girlfriend."

"Your girlfriend? How come you have all the luck?"

Edmond smiled and placed one hand on my shoulder.

"Sarah, meet Joe Benny. We are here for his father," Edmond said, turning towards the blonde-haired man. "Joe, meet Sarah Barry, my girlfriend."

Joe fixed his eyes on me as if he was mesmerized. He took my hand and left a kiss at the back of my hand.

"You are such a beautiful lady, Sarah. Arguably the most beautiful lady in this hall."

"Thank you," I replied, blushing.

"I have a feeling I would really enjoy speaking with you," Joe said, fixing himself in the empty chair beside me.

His interest looked sincere, but I wondered whether Edmond was comfortable with the way he looked at me.

We sat down together, but Joe was still holding on to my hand. Edmond hadn't noticed because he was thumbing on his phone.

"You are anxious," Joe whispered. I took a deep breath and smiled. He leaned closer and for a moment I thought he intended to kiss me.

"Be comfortable, Sarah. I have no sexual interest in you," he whispered, loosening his grip on my hand.

Joe kept his eyes on me and looked from my hair to the silver wristwatch on my wrist. He sniffed my hair.

"I know that smell. You use Klin shampoo?" Joe asked.

"Yeah. You figured that out by just smelling my hair?"

"You'd be surprised by how easily I figure things out," Joe responded, locking eyes with me for a moment.

I turned to Edmond and discovered that he had noticed Joe's intense attention on me.

"Joe is the marketing director of Benny publishing," Edmond said, with a smile.

This information struck me unusually. In that instant, I realized that I was sitting at the same table with a prospective publisher. I had intended to self-publish, but I realized that meeting Joe could be a turning point in my passion to become a writer.

I turned to Joe, who hadn't taken his eyes off me. He looked like a creep, but a creep wasn't supposed to smell so good.

"Can I talk to you about my book?" I asked.

"Your book? You're a writer?"

"I have been working on a novel for some time."

"This is starting to make sense."

"What?"

"Meeting you, Sarah. I'm an intuitive man."

I oscillated my eyes between Edmond and Joe. Joe, at this moment, sounded like Edmond on the very first day I met him.

"Well, I don't know what to say," I said.

"We can't talk about your book right here. Today should be for fun alone, but we can talk about it another time," Joe said, bringing out his business card.

He brought out a pen from the breast pocket of his suit and scribbled a number on the card.

"I don't want you to call my business line, it would take you to my PA. Call this number," he said, tapping the number he had just written down on the card.

"Thank you," I said, taking the card from him. I turned to Edmond. He was following our conversation.

"I'll be on my way now. My family must be growing impatient with my absence," Joe said, standing up. He smiled at me and walked away.

"He sounds like a really nice guy," I said, turning to Edmond.

"He looks like he really likes you," Edmond responded.

"He said he's not sexually attracted to me."

"Well, there are rumors that he's gay. Maybe the rumors are true."

"Did our conversation make you uncomfortable?" I asked.

"Nothing really looked out of place," Edmond responded, taking a sip of wine.

The sound of instruments pervaded the center. A rock band took center stage.

I turned to Mr. Evans. He was leaning towards his wife and whispering something in her ear.

Linda remained calm and relaxed, hiding the dangerous side I had seen at Blinks.

I was uncomfortable again and wished Joe had stayed behind. I couldn't deny the refreshment that his presence gave to me. He was the only one, apart from Edmond, that was genuinely interested in me. Perhaps it was just a skill he possessed. Perhaps it was the reason he was the marketing director of Benny Publishing.

After the performance of the band, Mr. Benny was accompanied to the stage by Joe. A round of applause swept through the center. I joined in, clapping as hard as I could. I didn't know Benny, but I knew and liked Joe.

Joe stood beside his father as he took the mic and welcomed the guests to the party.

"When I was thirty, I told myself that if I got to seventy, I was going to celebrate my birthday in a grand way. You see, a crazy lady had read my palm in the university. She said I'd die by sixty-eight," Benny said, cracking up the guests.

"Sixty-eight was a terrible year for me. I kept remembering what that lady said. But today, I realized that by giving her my palm to read, I let her have power over me," Benny said, taking a step forward.

"Today, I'm strong and I have enjoyed a fruitful marriage with my wife, Edna. We've been blessed by a son and two daughters. I have gotten more blessings than I ever expected in this world. And most importantly, I was able to do things my way. With the help of Joe, we have made Benny publishing the biggest in the world."

A round of applause swept through the center. Benny took Joe's hand and pulled him forward, ensuring he stood at his side.

"I wrote a speech about Joe and his impact in my businesses, but I tore it outside the center. He already knows how I feel about him. So what's the point?" Benny asked, cracking up the guests.

"If I get to eighty, I'd talk about him. He has the mind of my father and has made me believe in reincarnation. That's all. Joe go down. Go join your mother," Benny said, tapping Joe's shoulder. A rapturous laughter swept through the crowd. The laughter was accompanied by cheers and clapping as Joe clambered down from the stairs.

I joined in the clapping. As the applause died down, I felt Edmond's hand on my hair.

"Why does it feel like Joe has left such a good impression on you?" Edmond asked.

"He actually sounds like a great guy."

"Ladies and gentlemen, welcome to my party. I am so happy to have you guys here. Drink, merry, and if you get so drunk, just let the stewards know. They'd drive you to your homes. Thank you. Thank you so much," Benny said, and walked off the stage.

The applause was loud. Everyone at our table applauded him. I could see that Benny was a lovable guy, who had, through the years, acquired the respect and admiration of the folks in the center. It was during the applause that I saw Mr. Evans smile genuinely.

The smile of Mr. Evans reminded me that every villain had a story where they were good and loving. Evans was able to smile and express happiness for the life of Benny, but he had, since his arrival at the table, given hints about his revulsion for my relationship with Edmond.

And as if to reify my stance, Evans stopped clapping, picked up his glass of wine, and took a sip. As he dropped his glass gently on the table, he looked towards me. There was no sign of the man that had shown obvious happiness in applauding Benny. Evans had a solemn, unfriendly look that forced me to look away from him.

I witnessed more thrilling performances. There was comedy, music, dance, and I managed to look away from Linda and her family throughout these performances.

Edmond and I were mostly uncommunicative. There was little we could say in the presence of Linda, who sat closely to Edmond. Edmond kept checking his phone and shaking his head.

I wanted to ask about it, but decided to stay out of it because it didn't really affect his mood at the table.

Suddenly, Evans stood up, dipped one hand in his pocket, and moved towards Edmond. As he stretched his hand towards Edmond, Edmond stood up, gallantly.

"I would like to have a brief word with you," Evans said, holding on to Edmond's hand.

Edmond turned to me and smiled.

"I will be right back, Honey."

I was nervous and didn't want him to leave, but I was afraid of offending Evans by insisting on having Edmond with me.

Mrs. Evans was focused on the performance in the center. It appeared she wasn't caught up in the game of Mr. Evans and Linda.

I took a deep breath as Edmond and Evans proceeded from the table. I took two quick gulps from my glass and filled it to the brim.

Moments later, Linda stood up from her chair and sat down in Edmond's chair. This move sent grim flushes up my spine.

"You must think you're winning, bastard," Linda said.

"Stop calling me that."

"All poor people are bastards for all I care."

"I am not poor."

"Yes, you are. No one knows your family."

"You must really feel bad that a poor girl is perfect for your ex."

"Don't kid yourself, Bitch. You don't know what you're up against. You've not seen the madness of Linda," she said, emptying her glass in my dress.

I shifted away from her, shocked by this move. I took a quick look around the table. I wanted to see whether anyone had noticed her.

Unfortunately, everyone else was focused on the performance on stage.

"You are crazy," I said, taking out my hanky from my bag. I wiped some of the wine off my dress and kept my eyes on her.

"You have no idea, Sarah. When I'm crazy, the world listens," Linda said, refilling her glass.

pushed my chair backward and stood up, quickly. Linda remained in her chair and sipped from her glass.

I was afraid of sitting back in my chair because I knew she was going to pour more wine on my dress.

I thought about calling Edmond and reporting the issue to him. Surprisingly, Linda stood up with her glass of wine. She had that terrible, mad look. And I was afraid she was going to embarrass me in front of everyone.

"Everything has an end, Sarah. You think you can take what belongs to me?" Linda asked, raising her glass upward.

From the look in her eyes, I had a feeling she was going to aim for my face this time.

Fortunately, Michelle walked towards Linda from behind me. I looked around and found that Linda had attracted a bit of attention.

It was a bit surprising to see Michelle in the party. She had indicated that she had no intention of attending the party.

"What do you think you're doing?" Michelle asked. Linda smiled and moved back to her seat without responding to Michelle's question.

Michelle sighed and turned towards me. She rested one hand on my shoulder.

"Thank God you came in time," I said, gratefully.

"I have been watching you from my table."

"I thought you weren't coming."

"I changed my mind. I know. I'm doing that quite often these days."

"I feel like going home. I don't feel this party anymore."

"You can't keep letting her have so much power over you. You can't let her intimidate you."

"What am I going to do?"

Michelle turned to Linda and returned her gaze to me, quickly.

"Avoid her if you can, but if you can't, you have to fight her. She'll keep coming unless you do something."

"I just want to go home."

"No. Come. Come sit with me. There is a spare seat at my table," Michelle said, taking my hand.

I swiveled at Linda and met a big smile on her face. She raised her glass up and stuck out her tongue. Linda showed no restraint in doing this in the presence of everyone.

I was disenchanted with the party as Michelle walked me to her table. To be fair, I didn't think I could fight Linda. I couldn't afford to be so crazy in the presence of everyone. My job depended on it. My life depended on it.

Perhaps if I had the same privilege as her, I would have been able to return the sickening insult of emptying her glass on my dress.

I looked around the center and couldn't find Edmond.

At Michelle's table, I took out my phone and sent Edmond a text:

I want to go home. Please come take me home.

"You need to talk to Edmond about her. He needs to do something about it," Michelle admonished.

"I don't think it'll be easy for him. There is a madness in Linda that Edmond is running away from."

"Then you shouldn't be in the same party as her. Edmond has to make sure of that."

A round of applause pervaded the center, spelling the end of the performance of the band on stage. I hadn't followed the band at all and didn't intend to follow any other activity in the party.

My current state of mind expressed the victory of Linda, but I didn't think I needed to win her to achieve my goals and objectives. I didn't think I needed to resort to crude and childish exhibitions.

Edmond was the prize, and I would always be ahead of Linda as long as he kept to his promise of fighting for our relationship.

XVII

EDMOND

Evans walked weirdly beside me, quiet as he continued to lead me away from our table.

He stopped at a table and exchanged pleasantries with a few couples, encouraging me to do the same.

Afterwards, he rested his hand on my shoulder and continued forward. I was patient with him, but I wished he wouldn't stray too far from our table.

"Is this about business?" I asked, finally.

"What is not about business, Ed? Everything is about business. Even the wars we've fought are about business."

"Is this a good time?"

Evans stopped, took his hand from my shoulder, and faced me.

"You didn't notice? You didn't notice the tension at our table?"

"Tension?"

"Yeah. Between Linda and Sarah."

"Sarah is a sweet, innocent lady. She just wants to enjoy the party."

"That's what you think. You're a man, Ed. And sometimes men make the mistake of thinking that women think like us. That's not true."

"I ended things with Linda long before I met Sarah. She had no problem until Sarah was in the picture."

"Exactly. Women think differently. Linda always believed that you two are still together."

"Even while we were apart?"

"Yeah. It was only recently I learnt of your unfortunate breakup. Linda was in tears. She wouldn't eat unless I talked to you."

"Sarah is the picture now. There's nothing I can do."

"No. Don't say that. Pictures are erased and pictures are retaken. That's life, Son."

"I don't understand where this is going."

"I understand. You don't have a child yet. So you may not understand the pain of seeing your daughter cry herself to sleep night after night."

"I'm sorry about that, but…"

"Don't be sorry, Ed. Fix it. I was thinking about investing in your father's estate, but I have had a great offer from Steward. I am the only reason we don't have a merger to upset the position your father has taken in the industry."

"Is this a threat?"

"This is reality. This is the fact. I have put off that offer because I care about your future. I have always been under the impression that it is with my daughter."

"My father has seen off so many competitions in this industry. It is big enough for everyone to succeed."

"You don't see the big picture. The smaller you get, the easier it would be to absorb you."

"That cannot happen. Do you even understand the business of our industry?"

"You want to teach me business now? Who do you think your shareholders are aligned with? Dogs eat dogs, Son. It is a cruel world."

"I can't believe you're saying this."

"I have known your father for a long time, Ed. He is a good man. Maybe that's why I yearn for a son-in-law that is just as good."

"Linda is pretty. She can find another man easily."

"You are the one she wants. You are the one that makes her cry at night."

"I see. I respect you, Mr. Evans, but I can't believe you'd treat me so disrespectfully."

"Get a grip of yourself, Son. This is business."

"No. You brought me here to blackmail me so you can give me as a present to your daughter. You talk about dogs eating dogs... Maybe Linda would have been better if she didn't see life that way."

"You're in no position to tell me how to raise my daughter. But listen, I called you here to strengthen ties. I know how to make offers that people can't resist."

Evans inhaled deeply and ran one hand through his hair.

"Think about it, Son. You don't want to be in a future where you're forced to look back in anger," Evans added, and tapped my shoulder.

Incidentally, my phone beeped. I took it out from my pocket and found a text from Sarah. She wanted to go home.

It was an awkward text. At first, I wondered whether my absence had made her lonely, but then I remembered that Linda was at the table with her.

I hurried down to the table. Evans stopped at another table and greeted the folks at the table, cheerfully.

I didn't find Sarah at the table when I got there. Linda had a bright smile on her face.

"Where is Sarah?" I asked.

"Sit down. Let's talk about us," Linda responded.

"Where is Sarah?"

"I'm right here." Sarah's voice was sad and hushed. She was standing behind me, her face loomed down. I embraced her, tightly.

"What's the problem?" I asked.

"Let's speak in the car."

"You really want to go home?"

"Yes."

I took her hand and left the center with her. I had no intention of staying in the party without her.

We sat in the car, quiet for some time.

"What really happened?" I asked, finally.

"How were you able to cope with Linda?"

"What did she do?"

"Why does she believe she will win you back?"

"What did she do?"

"She poured her wine on my dress. I had to leave the table."

"I'm sorry. I'm so sorry. I shouldn't have left you alone with her."

"It's okay. It's not your fault. I still had a great day. I spent time with you."

"I'll make sure this doesn't repeat itself."

"How are you going to do that?"

I took a deep breath and placed one hand on my face. I couldn't stand the look on Sarah's face. There was no hint of joy on her face. Linda had succeeded in draining Sarah with her madness.

"You shouldn't be in this situation. There's so much at stake…you shouldn't have to suffer because of it."

"I am not suffering. What's at stake?"

For a moment I thought about telling her about the threats of Evans and his evil desire to target my father's company. I looked into her eyes and felt she didn't deserve to bear such a burden.

"It's okay. I'll figure it out. Let me drive you home."

"Why don't you want to talk about it?"

"It's just business."

XVIII

SARAH

Monday was normally supposed to be stressful, but I was already tired before afternoon. My mind was flood with roaming thoughts about my relationship with Edmond. I tirelessly tried to remain focused, but I couldn't pay attention. I decided to stop working.

I got up from my chair and walked towards the window. Sometimes I found staring at ordinary people from the fourteenth-floor liberating, as it offered refreshment to my frequent mental exhaustion.

I met a couple at the roadside. They were tiny from up here, but I could see they were holding hands as they strolled down the street. As the waited for the traffic light to turn green, the lady rest her head against the man's shoulder. Suddenly, I started to wish I could enjoy this sort of stroll with Edmond.

I turned away from the window and looked towards my desk. Impulsively, I picked up my phone:

How about we take a stroll later in the evening, Babe? This is the most beautiful Monday I've seen in a long time.

After sending the text, I dropped my phone back on the desk and rest my hands on the desk. I kept my eyes on my phone, waiting for his response.

I had no doubt in my mind that Edmond was going to agree to it. He had, since returning to me, made concerted moves in beautifying our relationship.

After five minutes of waiting, different stories started to pop up in my head, and if it was any consolation, it was fair to think that he wasn't around his personal phone during work hours.

I walked back to the window and looked towards to the road again.

I wanted to concentrate on the small beauty rapped through the road, but overthinking took over. Actually, the thoughts had already been on my mind, but I became wholeheartedly engulfed with paranoia.

There had to be a logical reason why Edmond hadn't responded to my text yet. To jump to the conclusion that the reason was because he wanted to withdraw from his relationship with me was terrible, but I couldn't help it.

It felt like my body had affected a procedure that intended to break my heart before Edmond eventually did. Perhaps it was my mind's way of fortifying my resolve in advance.

In any case, it was a terrible condition that left me mingling with thoughts that created the impression that Edmond had just broken up with me with his silence.

It took a while before it dawned on me that I wasn't even looking at the road anymore. I was closeted in my mind and focused on the bitter trajectory of my thoughts.

I moved from the window and quickly checked my phone. I had a feeling that Edmond might have responded to my message. There were times I had received messages without my phone making its usual beeping sound.

However, there was no message from Edmond. I dropped down in my chair, sat back, and shook my head.

As I was thinking about calling him, a knock came on my office door. Michelle came in and stood in the doorway.

"You brought lunch from home?" she asked.

"No."

"Come on. Let's go eat."

I stood up, reluctantly, and followed her to the cafeteria.

We had pancakes and coffee and were mostly uncommunicative. I was half-confined in my mind and forced myself to eat. It was a struggle to simply raise my arm to feed myself and every bite of pancake came with its own chewing difficulty. What I would have deemed pleasurable in the past felt like an impossible and mundane chore.

I managed to eat two pancakes, abandoning the third one as I sat back in my chair.

Michelle had already finished eating her pancakes. She was focused on her phone as she drank from her cup of coffee.

"Have you heard from Linda since yesterday?" Michelle asked.

"No. I wasn't expecting to hear from her."

"I think you should. She is a desperate woman and I think she'll try to get your number."

"I am not sure I'm going to let her get away with any embarrassing move again."

"You shouldn't. You don't have to but I'm hoping Ed would speak to her."

"I don't think that's a good idea. Ed is really strong, but he looks really weak around Linda. He looks like he's afraid of her."

"That is to be expected. Ed would know what she's capable of."

"I think there's more to this. Ed keeps saying there is so much at stake."

Michelle arched her face up thoughtfully and took a deep breath.

"Have you tried to ask him if there's more to it?"

"I have tried. He looks stressed and tired, but he still wouldn't talk about it."

"Maybe he doesn't want you to worry about what's bothering him."

"Isn't that what a relationship is supposed to be about? Besides, I am already worrying. I feel something is up."

"Don't worry until you have sufficient evidence that there's something wrong. Don't let yourself suffer twice."

"I didn't think it would be so difficult to enjoy a relationship. It just feels like I have to condone bits of misery to enjoy it."

"It's not always like that. Things can become even more beautiful. I think a relationship becomes stronger once a couple starts overcoming setbacks."

"I don't know what to do. Do you really think I can spend the rest of my life with Ed? Do you think we have a chance? Do you think something would stop us?"

Michelle gave me a puzzled, concerned look.

"You are overthinking this. It would solve nothing, trust me. Whether I believe in the two of you or not is not the point. You have to watch him. You have to know when to stay and when to walk away. But you must know that nothing is impossible. You love him. I think he loves you too. I think that's the most important thing at the end of the day."

I was consoled by Michelle's words, but to be honest I was still thinking about the lack of response to my text.

I took out my phone and checked again on our way out of the cafeteria.

Michelle was on her phone. It looked like a business call, and she was totally immersed in it. She stopped at the elevator door and waved me away.

I spent the rest of the day, oscillating between work and thoughts. I was bothered, but I was still able to do a bit of work.

In my apartment, I decided to watch a movie after taking a bath and freshening up.

I felt better after the bath. I helped myself to a meal of pasta and sat in front of my TV searching for something that would cheer me up. I found a highly rated romance movie and tried my best to focus on it. Surely the script writers would give the movie a happy ending…

My phone was on the living room table. Infrequently, I turned to it, expectant.

Although it was an enjoyable movie, I didn't follow it with the keen interest I usually utilized. I was able to keep up with the story while missing out on most of the small, important things.

Mannerisms, especially, was a trait I looked out for in the characters. Although I didn't plan to be a script writer, I wanted to be stronger in conveying the emotions of my characters in the novel I was working on.

My pasta was delectable. I didn't have to contend with a jaded palate throughout. After I finished eating, I paused the movie and walked down to the kitchen.

I did the dishes, maintaining a habit of keeping my kitchen clean.

My phone screen was on when I returned to the living room. I hurried down to the table, picked it up, and discovered that it was a notification from Snapchat. A new, unknown contact had just sent a snap.

I didn't bother to look at the snap. I was disappointed. I resumed the movie, but my concentration level became worse.

I didn't think it made sense that Edmond hadn't responded to my message at this time. It was already 8:47pm.

I started to wonder if something terrible had happened to him. I shaved off this thought, realizing that if something had happened, the news would already be widespread, and Michelle would have apprised me of it.

What if he's just a bit ill from all the stress of yesterday? My mind asked.

I decided to call him. The impulse was strong inside me. Moments away from dialing his number, his text popped up on my phone screen. The coincidence surprised me and brought a smile on my face.

I sat back in my chair, anticipating a great, poetic text. I unlocked my phone and met:

Sorry for the slow reply. There's been a lot on my mind. I think we may need to take things slow - we'll talk more when I next see you.

Talk more about what?? What is on his mind? It suddenly felt like I had lost the ability to breathe. My nostrils were blocked, and sickening fluids of fear ran inside me.

I felt hot and sick. My vision became blurry, and it felt like my entire body was imploding.

I had to resort to measured huffs and puffs, but it wasn't enough. I felt a headachy sensation at the back of my head and the room started to spin ever so slightly. It felt like I was going to pass out, but I fought myself to remain conscious. I could hear the sound of my breathing.

I lay back down, stretching my body as I kept my eyes on the ceiling. This was an unprecedented experience and as my heart started to palpitate intensely, I feared that I was going to die. I feared that I would succumb to a cardiac arrest and just die.

As I lay down, thinking about death, I wondered how long it would take for anyone to find me if I died suddenly in my living room.

I reckoned Michelle would check up on me if I didn't show up at work tomorrow, but she was probably the only person who would.

I could die in my living room and not receive any attention until my corpse became quite rotten and drained the hallway in a vicious smell. Perhaps my neighbors would ignore the smell because of their busy schedule. Perhaps this room would be my cemetery until my bank account stopped taking the automatic debit for my rent.

This realization filled me with fear as my heart continued to drum inside me.

I closed my eye as this helped in reducing the headache at the back of my head.

I remained in that position for a long while as I tried to find stability in my thought and body.

In this bitter struggle, my mind was disconnected from the text of Edmond. Surprisingly, it was the memory of my shopping experience with Michelle at Top Luxury that came to the forefront of my mind.

I started to smile as I lay back and kept my eyes open. Gradually, my temperature became normal. My breathing became better.

My auditory sense became open to the sound of the movie pervading the living room. Reality became emboldened.

The sweet memory with Michelle fizzled out. My mind and body had become strengthened, and the text of Edmond reverberated inside me.

There were no tears in my eyes, but I knew I was sad. Perhaps I had chanced upon a different kind of sadness that killed off expressions and hid itself so thoroughly.

I stood from the chair and turned off the TV. I walked down to the kitchen and took a glass of water. I felt the water slide down my throat as cold shivers enveloped my body. My knees became weak as if they were tired of carrying my own body.

I walked to my room and dropped face down in my bed, draping myself over with a duvet as I tried to catch some sleep.

XIX

SARAH

It was easy to pretend, to keep my mind fixed on other things. I was desperate to keep sadness away from my mind. I found a way, an intelligent way, to squeeze in sound, consolatory thoughts.

I was able to maintain this rhythm and process till the weekend. Somehow, I had made myself believe that Edmond's silence was not a reflection of the text I had received from him on Monday evening.

I immersed myself in the delusion that he was simply going through a process, the same process that had made him pull away from me at the start of our relationship.

I knew better, but the benefits of ignorance were crucial to the sustenance of my mental health. I needed to detach myself from rational thoughts to exude some semblance of joy. It felt like madness. It felt like something about the text had turned a screw in my brain.

A message from Michelle popped up on my phone.

I'm outside.

Michelle had invited me to a kayaking contest in Pomona. She was leaning against her Cadillac and eagerly tapping away on her phone when I stepped out of the elevator lobby.

"I thought you hadn't read my text. I was thinking about coming up there," Michelle said.

"I was already on my way down. I didn't see the need to reply," I blurted. My eyes were fixed on Michelle and I noticed the slight change in her expression.

In the car, she sat back and turned towards me. I was looking away from her, but I knew she was focused on me. I knew my response to her text was slightly cold.

"Is there a problem?" she asked.

"Problem? No."

"Don't lie to me, Sarah. You don't look alright."

"Why would you say so? I look great. Just that I've been waiting for you for some time."

"That can't be. I arrived five minutes early."

"Oh! Really?" I asked, checking my silver wristwatch.

"Tell me what the problem is."

"There is no problem."

"Is it Edmond? Has he started behaving weird again?"

I was quiet and needed to choose my next words carefully. In that instant, reason and emotion collided, and I struggled to find the right answer to her question.

It was when I felt Michelle's hand on my shoulder that I realized that I had taken too long to assign an answer to her question.

"What happened? When last did you hear from him?" Michelle asked.

"I think he's going through some challenges. He's troubled. There's something up, but he doesn't want to talk about it."

"Haven't we talked about this? Focus on what you see. As long as he still treats you like the only one that matters, allow him to take his time. When the time is right, he's going to let you in."

I looked at Michelle and knew immediately that the time had come to tell her the truth. I had been so strong but as our eyes locked, I felt my cheeks burn as a tear glide down.

"What's the problem? Why are you crying?"

That one tear held the key to the floodgate, and its unlocking power caused my eyes to well up.

"Ed sent a text on Monday evening. He wants us to take things slowly."

"What does slowly mean?"

"I don't know."

"Have you spoken to him ever since?"

"No."

"No?"

"He hasn't called. I told him I'd like to go out on a stroll with him before he said that."

Michelle pressed her lips together and placed one hand on her forehead.

"Do you know what that means?" she asked.

"Please don't say anything. He's going through a hard time. This has happened before."

"The problem with tolerating bad behavior is that people would keep treating you that way. They won't stop. They won't stop unless you stop tolerating it."

"I think there's more to it," I retorted.

"It's okay. There is more to it. Of course there is but he wants you guys to take things slowly after starting off fast. You don't see anything wrong with that?"

I sniffled and swooped my face down. I was fraught with regret and dismay. I didn't think Michelle had the patience to see Edmond the way I saw him. I was vulnerable to my feelings for Edmond, which eased my way towards tolerance.

"I just feel things will go back to normal. Remember what you said? Remember? You said a couple becomes stronger from overcoming adversity."

Michelle shook her head, pitiably. Her eyes were wet and she looked at me as if I had lost my mind.

"That's not the point, Sarah. What's the point of overcoming adversity if you're the only one trying to overcome it?"

I was shaken by her question and dropped back in my chair. Michelle's presence made it difficult to cling onto the delusion that had kept my mind and heart from harm's way. It felt like I had just received the bitter message from Edmond all over again.

"Don't think too much about it, Sarah. After kayaking, I'll take you to dinner. We'll talk more there."

"I think I see why you wouldn't give in to any man," I said.

"Don't be pessimistic. You're great the way you are. I really believe things will get better for you."

"You really do?" I asked.

Michelle nodded, pressing her lips together. Her nod was halfhearted and gave me the impression that she simply didn't want me to sink deeper in the cesspit of sadness.

"You will be alright whether you have him or not. Remember you've done so well on your own," Michelle admonished.

I shook my head and looked away from her.

Michelle turned away from my apartment as I looked through the window at my side. Edmond's presence had left me with incredibly beautiful feelings, but in retrospect, these feelings had become thorns in my heart. It felt like he had been sent by fate to teach me a lesson. It felt like I wouldn't be able to find the desire to love again if Edmond walked out of my life.

The Riley Lake in Pomona was the most attractive part of the park, which spanned across 450 acres of land. The road leading from the gate to the lake was flanked by tall trees with overhanging foliage. The trees offered a comforting freshness and gave the lake the ambiance of a countryside.

Michelle pulled up at the parking lot which was beside a one-storied building that overlooked the lake. Low and behold, Ed's car was parked in the parking lot. I didn't know if I was excited or scared to potentially bump into him.

There were throngs of people at the park and around the bank of the lake. Subconsciously, I kept a look out for Ed amongst the crowd.

The folks were conversational and organized. There was no terrible exhibition, and it looked like these were a different breed of people from the one I met at Blinks Center.

When the faces started to become familiar, it started to dawn on me that these people exuded different feelings and behaviors in different places. I met Smith and his spouse. They held hands and were romantically huddled up.

Smith looked towards me and looked away quickly before I could wave at him. Smith dropped his face and his spouse turned towards me. She looked slightly nervy before she looked away.

I felt Michelle's hand on my wrist and looked away from Smith and his spouse.

"Remember we need to win this one. I have never won the contest," Michelle said, keeping her face forward.

Although I heard her clearly, I was thinking about Smith's weird behavior and wondered whether I should have gone to meet and greet him.

"Are you listening to me?" Michelle asked.

"Yeah."

"You said you have experience in kayaking?"

"Yeah. I'm pretty good at it."

"Then I think we really have a chance. My last teammate was really terrible. I did all the work."

Michelle tapped my shoulder and jerked me off my mind.

"I hope you're not thinking about the text?"

"No. I just have a weird feeling that something is not right."

"Well, I get that at times, but there's no need to dwell on it."

Michelle and I walked into the building that overlooked the lake and went to the ladies' changing room.

There was a big locker-room section before the door that led to the restroom. Walled-in benches jutted out from underneath the locker-rooms.

As I brought out my swimsuit, the door leading to the restroom creaked open.

Linda came out of the restroom in a pink swimsuit. Her brown hair was tied in a bun, and her face was smooth. Linda had a smile on her face and placed her hands on her waist as soon as she met me.

Did they come here together?

I was slightly anxious and thought she would come for me. Michelle noticed and looked up at Linda, who remained quiet as she looked in our direction.

Linda shook her head and started to walk away.

"Row, row, row, your boat, gently down the stream, merrily, merrily, merrily, merrily, life is not a dream," Linda sang loudly, as she laughed and walked out of the room.

"Something must be really wrong with her," Michelle said seriously.

"She sounded victorious," I responded under my breathe.

"Does it matter? It's not like you're fighting with her. I've seen enough to understand why Edmond left her."

"I feel really weird, Michelle."

"Don't let her get into your head."

"Why didn't she try to fight me or say something nasty?" I feared I had already lost the war.

"Oh. Come on. Don't think about it. It will not make you feel better."

"But I can't help it."

"You can and you have to try."

I dropped both hands on my face, frustrated by the trajectory of my week.

Moments later, we changed into our swimsuits, locked up our dresses in a locker-room, and proceeded to the lake.

Outside the building, Michelle took out her phone from a small bag weaved around her waist.

"Let's take a selfie, Sarah. I'm not sure we have enough pictures together."

She weaved one arm around my shoulder and stretched her phone forward. I feigned a smile, as her phone clicked repeatedly.

As Michelle dropped her phone in her bag, I saw Linda and Edmond at the other side of the building. Although I had already predicted they may be here together, I felt completely different seeing it in reality. The only word that could describe how I felt in that moment was broken. I really had lost the battle.

As I continued to I look towards them at the corner of my eye, Linda whipped out her phone and started taking snapshots.

Edmond was looking towards her phone, fully involved. He actually smiled a few times. Linda looked towards us and stuck out her tongue as she took another snapshot.

Edmond followed her line of vision and immediately drew apart from her. He was fraught with guilt and looked like he was thinking about coming to meet me.

From behind him, Linda curled her hands around his neck and pulled him close, leaving small kisses on his cheek. Edmond dropped his face as she kissed him.

I felt Michelle's hand on my shoulder.

"Be calm," she whispered.

My breathing became heavy. My hands trembled and I felt a terrible vibration inside me. It felt like I was closing in on a repeat of the emotions and condition that afflicted me after receiving Edmond's text, only this time I had a bit of experience. I tried to breath, relying on loud huffs and puffs.

Linda was still standing in my line of vision with Edmond, but I couldn't see them clearly as my vision became fuzzy from the tears gathered in my eyes.

"I need to go home," I said, turning to Michelle. She nodded and held on closely. "Let me take you home," she added, leading me to her car.

Michelle opened the door for me and watched me from outside as I sat back in the passenger's seat in front.

"I'll just go get our bags and dresses," she added, and closed the door.

As I waited for Michelle, I tried to keep my mind away from the harsh reality of seeing Linda and Edmond together. Only, it was difficult. I couldn't pretend to downplay the seriousness of their union. It started to feel like I was the one trying to put them asunder. I was the situation they needed to overcome to become stronger.

XX

SARAH

Michelle wouldn't take her eyes off me. She was worried and I was mad with myself for being needy and putting her in a position of discomfort.

She sat beside me in the living room, turning on the TV, desperate to find a distraction from my experience at the lake.

I was no longer impelled to cry. Instead, I felt numb. It felt like a large part of myself had died. I was stuck in my mind and literally thought about dying.

I looked towards the window and wondered if jumping through it and dying would make the news. Would he care enough then? I visualized myself walking down to the window and cutting off the barricade suffused in it. I knew it would be harder to cut off the barricade. The builders clearly intended to prevent sudden defenestration.

"Do you want to eat something? I could go buy you anything. Just name it."

"I am okay."

"You are not okay, Sarah and it's okay to not be okay. A lot of people are not okay, but you can't solve your problems by avoiding them."

"What do you want me to do? There is nothing to solve."

"I want you to live, Sarah. I want you to live with the greatest intensity. I know you are heartbroken, but I have come to realize that pain is a part of life. We can try to minimize it, but we have to understand that it's always going to be around. It's always going to try and find a way."

"I am going to live, Michelle, but I don't think I'll really enjoy it."

"And that's alright as well. You can't always enjoy life but there are going to be beautiful moments that you don't want to miss. Those moments will always come but we cannot allow our sadness to get in the way."

"I wish it was this easy. I wish someone could come and just erase all our memories. I wish I could just forget that I ever knew him."

"I am so sorry, Sarah. I really thought this could work. I really thought you two were perfect together."

"Do you think Linda is blackmailing him? Do you think that's what's at stake? Maybe that's why he can't tell me?"

Michelle shook her head and leaned closer, stroking my hair.

"Don't try to rationalize it. It will only make things worse."

"But don't I deserve to know why he doesn't want me anymore? Is it because I'm not from a wealthy home?"

Michelle took a deep breath and stood up from her chair. She picked up the TV remote and switched off the TV. She sat on the table and turned to me.

"You're perfect, Sarah. There's nothing wrong with you at all. I have never had a friend like you. You have everything any friend would wish for."

"Do you think we are cursed? Maybe we are not supposed to find real love in this world."

Tears started to well up in Michelle's eyes. She opened her mouth to say something, but quickly closed it back. Her lips quivered and she dropped one hand on her forehead. She looked away from me and towards the window.

Michelle moved the back of her right hand across her face, wiping off her tears.

I felt terrible. I was sad and befuddled, but making Michelle sad worsened the way I felt about myself. Since meeting Edmond, I had been unable to control my feelings and it had rubbed off on Michelle unpleasantly.

"I need a drink. I'll just go buy a bottle of wine and..."

"There is wine in the kitchen," I retorted. "And pancakes too."

Michelle took another deep breath and stood up from the table.

"Let me bring them," I said, standing up.

"No. I'll do it." Michelle smiled and went to the kitchen.

Michelle remained in the kitchen for a while, which got me worried. As I walked to the kitchen, Michelle came out. She stood in the doorway holding the bottle of wine and two glasses. She had a smile on her face, but there were bleary splotches in her eyes.

"Come on. Let's drink," she said, walking past me.

She kept her face down as she returned to the living room. She served the two glasses, filling them to the brim. Blobs of wine slobbered off the brim of the second glass, which she handed to me as I stood beside her.

"I'm sorry," I said.

"What? Why are you sorry? You didn't do anything," Michelle said, taking a sip.

"I am making you sad and it's not fair."

"No. No. Don't be like that. You need me now, okay? What are friends for?"

"I always need you, Michelle. I don't think it's fair."

"Nah. You don't know what you do for me? You're an amazing friend. Please don't start. Take a drink."

I took a drink and sat down. Michelle sat beside me and picked up the remote, resuming the movie we were watching.

The time was edging past 7:50pm, but Michelle, surprisingly, showed no signs of leaving. We were in our second movie, and although I was barely watching, I enjoyed her company.

At 8:20pm, I went to the kitchen and returned with another bottle of wine.

Michelle looked up at me with constricted eyes, stretching her glass towards me.

"You are driving, Michelle. This is dangerous."

"Who says I'm driving?"

"Aren't you driving home?"

"Not tonight. I'm staying with you tonight."

I was surprised by her utterance, but Michelle had actually given me another hint of the importance of my friendship to her.

"I don't... Shouldn't you... Wouldn't there..."

"You don't have to say anything, Sarah. Unless you don't have space for me in your apartment."

"No. No. Of course I have enough room for you. It's just..."

"Then that's enough. That's all I want to hear. Now pour me some wine."

I opened the bottle and served her glass. Her words and the position she had taken in my grief made me feel better. To feel loved and appreciated by Michelle wasn't something I could take for granted. It was a sign that I wasn't so unlucky.

The smile didn't come, but I was able to focus on the movie. The realization that I wouldn't be spending the night alone in my apartment was liberating.

We were uncommunicative, but I turned towards Michelle infrequently. I met her eyes a few times. The red splotches weren't as intense.

My phone vibrated suddenly. I turned to Michelle and met her eyes. I had a feeling we were both thinking the same thing.

I picked up my phone and found a text from Edmond:

I made promises and I feel like a fool. We should talk, Sarah. Just to talk. Nothing else. I am outside your apartment building. I know I've made you sad. But let's just talk. I will wait for 30 minutes.

The cheek.

After reading the message in my mind a few times, I read it out loud.

"What's wrong with him??" Michelle asked.

"I don't know. I think I made a mistake. I should have taken my time to study him."

"You didn't have a choice, Sarah. It was love at first sight, remember?"

"What do you think I should do? Should I go down and speak with him?"

"Follow your heart. I support any decision you take."

I took a sip of wine, dropped my glass heavily, and shook my head. At this point, I was desperately mad at him, but I had a sneaky feeling that Edmond was confused and miserable.

I stood from the chair and paced around the living room.

Michelle turned down the volume of the TV and stood up.

"If you want to speak with him, go down and speak with him. It's okay to be a fool until you lose your feelings for him."

Michelle spoke like an old woman that had seen it all in life.

"I am going to speak with him, but I don't think I can refuse him if he wants us back again."

"Refusing him would be good for your esteem, but if you want to take him back, at least demand for an explanation. You deserve to know why he has been behaving weirdly. If there's no explanation, you'll be foolish to take him back."

I nodded, took a deep breath, and started towards the bathroom.

"Sarah," Michelle called, walking towards me. She handed me my phone. "Just in case you take him back and need to go on a ride with him," Michelle added, smiling.

I felt slightly embarrassed as I took the phone from her hand. Michelle gave me a warm embrace.

"Don't be hard on yourself."

I walked to the bathroom and stood in front of the mirror. I looked a mess. My eyes were puffy, and the blood vessels in my eyes were prominent, like well-lit Christmas lights that encased my iris. I splashed cold water on my face and gargled mouthwash to get rid of the strong smell of wine on my breathe. I tied my hair up into a high bun and wiped off any remnants of pancakes from my clothes.

As I stepped out of the elevator lobby, Edmond was standing outside his mustang, with his hands dipped in his pockets. I remembered the moment he had run towards me in the doorway of the lobby. This time, Edmond remained beside his car. It gave me the impression that he hadn't come to try and win me back.

I kept my eyes on him as I walked towards him. I stopped two yards away from him and folded my arms against my breast.

He took an awkward breath and kept wiping his face with the back of his hand. His face was flushed, and he descended into a routine of taking his hands from his pocket and dipping them back.

The silence between us made me emotional, but I tried to remain strong before him.

Sloughs of chilling breeze gusted past, and a rash gooseflesh rapped over my arms. Perhaps I should have dressed warmly before coming down to meet him.

"You said you wanted to talk."

"You should be mad at me. But I am not doing this for me...I'm doing this for other reasons."

"What other reasons, Ed? Why does it feel like you made an experiment on me?"

"No. No. That's not what I had in mind. I love you. I really do."

"You keep saying that. But you promised to show more actions. You said words were not enough. If you love me, you wouldn't have gone back to your ex. You would have tried to make things work between us."

"This is not my choice. I'm being forced to do this."

"What do you mean? Linda is blackmailing you?"

"It is more than that. Years of hard work is on the verge of being dismantled."

"Why aren't you telling me about what has caused this? You keep speaking in parables."

"You won't understand. To be fair, this is not your business. I shouldn't have involved you."

"I am tired of your apologies. It seems it's the only thing you're good at."

"No. I… I think you're right. I'm a disappointment to you. I failed you, but I can't stop loving you. I can't stop believing that we are meant to be."

"Oh! Please shut up. Just shut up. You saw a fool, Ed. You made her love you so you could break her heart. You came to my life to ruin me. What are you apologizing for? You've succeeded. Congratulations."

Tears trickled down from my eyes as I looked at him. The tears made my vision blurry.

"Goddamn it," Edmond bawled.

His voice was loud and forced me to wipe my tears.

"This is not my intention. I had good plans for us," he said.

"It doesn't matter anymore. Words are not enough."

I sniffled and took a look at his eyes. There were tears in them. Quickly, I looked away from him and hurried back to elevator lobby.

I reclined against a wall in the lobby and cried loudly. The silence in the lobby made it easy for me to cry as much as I needed. I watched Edmond's mustang through the open door of the lobby. I watched as he got back into his car and drove away from my apartment and out of my line of vision.

I knew life wasn't a fairytale, but I thought the man I love would have come running after me. I thought that the man that loves me would have fought for what we had, no matter what that meant. Yet here I was, alone in the lobby, crying ecstatically as if I was mourning the death of a loved one.

When the tears stopped rolling down my cheeks, I stepped into the elevator, but unfortunately, I could still hear his words in my mind. His voice was loud inside my head, and spontaneously, my mind tried to make sense of his words.

XXI

EDMOND

It was sadness I found at every corner of the road as I drove down to Pomona. I found sadness on the faces of the freelance guitarists at the roadside without no audience. Sadness reared itself conspicuously, and it wasn't the kind that made me cry.

I had tried to prevent this reality, but I didn't think I tried hard enough. Maybe, at the end of the day, I was a coward, afraid to take the necessary risks to be with the woman, in whom I had found love.

I managed to remain awake, but I was tired, weak, frustrated. Something inside me grew weaker the more I was away from Sarah.

In my father's estate, I stood outside my car and looked towards the mansion. At the top floor, there was a mini library that covered my family's ancestry. There was book containing the brief history of my family's occupation in California.

I was particularly influenced by the history of my family. Every Barker, dead and alive, had needed to take a great risk to sustain the wealth in the family. Maybe we were cursed to sacrifice true happiness for wealth.

As I looked towards the mansion, I wondered if I would regret this move. I wondered if my forefathers had equally contended with regret on their death beds.

I was at the point where living had lost the intensity that made it beautiful. Maybe it would have been better to make this sacrifice if I didn't meet Sarah.

I walked languidly to my duplex home. Some of Sarah's words resonated inside me. It wasn't the first time, but they reminded me of how stupidly I had managed my time with her.

Yards away from my home, I discovered that the entrance door was open. There was music wafting out of the living room.

I thought it was my father. It was certainly the kind of music he loved and preferred.

In the living room, I found Linda. She was a in a pink bikini top and white G-string panties. Her body was oiled and she held a glass of wine in one hand. She stretched out her hand and passed me the glass.

Although my mind was elsewhere, Linda's sexiness distracted me. She looked like a temptation straight from the devil. She stuck out her tongue and moved them circularly as she walked closer towards me. I gulped down the glass of wine immediately.

She rolled her tongue around my lips and took the glass of wine from my hand. She moved past me, locked the entrance door, and placed the empty glass onto a coffee table.

When Linda returned, she was holding her G-string panties in one hand. She wore it on my head and let it slide down my neck like a necklace.

I could perceive her vagina secretion in the gusset of her panties.

"I am so wet. I'm so crazy for you, baby," she said, leaning closer.

She grabbed her panties and turned the gusset to my face. Linda wanted to choke me with the smell of her secretion.

She leaned closer, sticking her tongue through an opening in her panties. I felt her tongue at the corner of my lips and felt the gusset at the other corner. As much as I didn't want to focus on her seduction, my body staved into it.

My dick had a different brain when it came to analyzing Linda's seduction. It was a temptation it was willing to embrace. The wetness of her tongue against my lips was enough to make my dick rise, and the smell of her panties made me ten times harder. I felt my dick hit the zippers of my jeans, desperate to answer Linda's call.

Linda, who had an unusually telepathic understanding with my dick, unzipped my jeans and grabbed my dick with authority. It was so sexy. She grabbed it hard and tight, as she continued to dip her tongue in and out of my mouth.

It was at this moment my sense of reason faded away. I was gripped by the impulse to sexually devour her. Sex, at this instant, seemed like a good way to rid myself of the misery from leaving Sarah.

In the depth of her seduction, Linda grabbed my shirt and guided me like a dog up the stairs to the top floor. She took me to our favorite room. It was the biggest room in the house. It had a king size bed, and the ceiling was completely covered by a glass mirror which reflected every inch of activity beneath it.

As we entered the bedroom, Linda ripped off my clothes. She pushed me onto the bed and slowly climbed on top of me, staring at me with her large beady eyes as if I was a three-course meal. She was in control, and I began to drool in anticipation of what was coming next.

Linda bounced her naked body up and down on my penis. Each thrust felt better than the last as I got deeper and deeper inside of her. As I looked up towards the mirror above us, her body looked as though it had been sculpted by the gods. I placed my hands on her round butt cheeks and slapped them hard.

She was relentless and the sound of moaning came like the sound of hymns from a Catholic church. The warmth of her body, the warmth beneath her legs, the warmth of her kisses, defined her rigorous talent in this endeavor. This was the sort of sex that destroyed kings, and it felt convenient at this moment.

Linda was destroying everything, my attachment to Sarah, the future I had envisaged with her. With every thrust and moan, I felt my head becoming muddled up. This felt like therapy.

And when I eventually came, she held me tightly, curling both her hands and feet around my body. Her breathing was heavy, my will was gone. Linda made sure I dropped my seeds inside her.

I dropped down and felt emotional. Ejaculation brought clarity. Linda was not supposed to be the one, and I wasn't supposed to be such a fool.

She continued to hold onto me long after I ejaculated. She kept my flaccid dick inside her and closed her eyes as if she wanted to cast a spell that would make both our privates inextricable.

Eventually, I pulled away from her and discovered that she had fallen asleep. I rolled to the other side of the bed and looked towards the ceiling.

I had failed myself, but I didn't think there was any need to dwell on it if I couldn't find a way to change this situation.

After a little while, I went to the bathroom and took a shower. It was a shower interspersed with diverse, humbling thoughts. I had been a genius in most things. I had made the best decisions in most of my occupations. Now, I was humbled by the reality that I was still capable of becoming a fool in spite of my flashes of brilliance.

Linda was still asleep when I returned to the bedroom. I wore a blue robe and went outside the room.

I clambered down the stairs and picked up the bottle of wine that Linda had left on the coffee table in the living room, taking large gulps straight from the bottle as I walked outside the house. I traipsed down to my father's mansion and met him in the porch at the entrance. He was sitting in a lounge chair and drinking from a glass.

He looked up at me and shook his head.

"What is it this time son?" he asked.

"My dreams. They bother me."

"The dream has always been to keep the business alive…"

"I have my personal dreams, Father. One of them is marrying a woman I love."

"But you love Linda. You said that yourself."

"Not anymore."

My father took a sip of whiskey and sighed, deeply.

"If your love for Linda could die so easily, why do you think the next lady is safe? It is not good to dwell on dreams Ed. Besides, I don't even understand the sort of love you're talking about. I don't understand the kind of love that dies so easily."

"Linda betrayed me. She deceived and manipulated me. I missed her while we were apart, but I was sure I didn't want to be with her anymore."

"You made a sacrifice son. Every one of us have made one."

"But how did we lose 45 percent of the company to shareholders??"

"It was a mistake on my part son. The shares were overvalued at the time. We wanted to make as much as possible to invest into renewable energy."

"I thought our company was untouchable."

"It still is, alright. If Evans wasn't partnering with Hutchinson and Steward, we would have mopped up the lost shares when the prices drop."

"You should have told me about it at least. You can't have me trying to create competition for our parent company when we are close to losing it."

"We are not close to losing it! Don't be dramatic."

"They intend to buy 45 percent of our company Dad. We gave them the opportunity."

"But you saved the day," he said, grabbing hold of my shoulder. "Now Evans intends to work with us. He has promised to put the ownership in Linda's name once you marry her. That keeps everything in the family."

"We shouldn't have been in this situation. You've literally ruined my life."

My father was quiet. He removed his hand away from me and shook his head slightly.

"We have been making this decision for some time. We've always been great at taking advantage of the market prices of our shares, but it is what it is. Listen, we are investing in other sectors. In the future, the Barker will be known for something else."

"But you should have told me Father... I don't think I'll ever truly be happy without Sarah."

My father dropped his face and glass of whiskey. He struggled to look up at me.

"I would ask you to follow your heart, but I don't trust the intention of Evans. This is the time we need to stick together as a family."

I took a deep breath and walked away from my father without uttering another word. I couldn't be mad at him because he made a simple transaction that had brought him success in the past.

Back in my duplex home, I turned off the music and returned to the top floor.

I met Linda sitting up in the bed. She was totally naked and had a big smile on her face.

"You couldn't stay with me while I tried to catch a break?" she asked, stepping out of the bed.

I took a deep breath as I regarded her firm, beautiful body. I felt cold flushes in my body.

Her right hand settled on my shoulder and she drew closer to me, rolling her tongue around her top lip. I had been in this situation several times, and Linda had usually succeeded in making me responsive to her moves.

She took my hand and raised the bottle to her lips. She took a gulp and swallowed slowly.

Afterward, she kissed me, sticking her tongue in my mouth and wiggling it.

She grabbed my penis, which, unashamedly, become hard again. Although her sex drive was insane, my body could never resist. She took charge again, initiating sexual positions that exposed her flexibility.

As she started to moan, I thought about Sarah. It was the first time I had managed this sort of thought during sex with her. I thought about the kiss I shared with Sarah outside Steward's home. I thought about the joy that filled my heart after spending time with her. I thought about the first time we made love...

I felt a slap on my face. Linda knew my mind was elsewhere.

"Look at me baby. Think about me. Think about us. Only us baby," she moaned.

Nonetheless, it was difficult to not think about Sarah. Linda's moves were impressive, her energy was intoxicating, and she was clearly desperate to enjoy this moment with me.

It became clear that in spite of Linda's effort, the enchantment from a second round wasn't as compelling as the first. In this round, I was able to think about other things, especially the things I had done to Sarah. And when I finally ejaculated, it felt like an excuse for Linda to let me think about Sarah without the interruption of her thrusts.

XXII

SARAH

Michelle was happy and unusually excited as we moved through the glass doors of Settlers.

Settlers was a beautiful, French restaurant, adorned with round tables and cushioned, straight-back chairs.

We settled at a table and Michelle picked up the menu, looking over the top at my face.

"Why are you smiling so much?" I asked.

"This means a lot to you. Come on. Joe will be here in twenty minutes."

"Yeah but he hasn't said that my book has been accepted by the editorial team."

"It has been two weeks since you submitted that book. You really think Joe would have waited this long if it didn't make sense?"

"This is the biggest publishing company in the US, Michelle. They have loads of books to attend to."

"Doesn't matter. I am sure they'd prioritize a book sent over by Joe."

An attendant walked down to our table, bowing and smiling.

"How may I serve you?" he asked.

"I'll have the croque-monsieur," Michelle said, excitedly. The attendant turned towards me with a smile.

"I'll have what she's having," I said.

I was a bit nervous, but I didn't intend to abandon my book if it was rejected by Benny publishing. I believed it was relevant in this era and suitable for all ages. Hence, I had plans to reconsider self-publishing if Joe returned with bad news.

I kept checking my timepiece. It was the silver wristwatch I had received from Edmond. I loved it in spite of the sad story behind it. It had been seven weeks since I received that heartbreaking text from Edmond.

"What's on your mind?" Michelle asked.

"I'm not really thinking. I'm keeping my mind open."

"I think you have done great for yourself. It's not easy to complete a book after such a terrible heartbreak."

"To be fair, the heartbreak helped. This might sound funny, but sadness makes me a better writer."

"Well, that doesn't mean you should yearn for it."

"I understand, but I will probably write another book if I get another traumatic experience."

"Well, maybe you need to work on using happiness as a fuel."

"We'll see about that."

The attendant returned with our order and placed them neatly on the table.

"Wine or Champagne?" he asked.

"Champagne," we responded, concurrently. Michelle giggled.

Incidentally, Joe walked into the restaurant. He wore a blue suit; his hair was curly and sleek. He had his phone against his ear and kept nodding as he walked towards our table.

"Ladies," he said, with a big smile. He took my hand and left a kiss on the back of my hand. Michelle stood up and embraced him.

I was nervous as I looked up at him, only I tried to hide my anxiety by smiling at him. He sat down in a chair, typing away on his phone.

The attendant returned with our champagne and bowed.

"I'd like a glass of champagne as well," Joe said, winking at the attendant before dropping his phone in his pocket.

"I am so sorry for postponing this meeting. I've been incredibly busy," Joe said.

"I understand," I replied.

"Well, what do you think of the book?" Michelle asked, cutting to the chase.

Joe smiled and sat up in his chair. The attendant returned with his glass of champagne.

Joe turned to me, pressing his lips together, and giving off a suppressed smile. I had an immediate sense that he had come with bad news.

"I thought about doing this virtually, but I feel it is something I need to do face to face," Joe said, taking a deep breath.

"It's okay. I am just starting out as a writer. I know I may not have everything figured out," I said, consoling myself in advance.

"Jesus Christ, Sarah. You really do need to work on your self-selling skills. You think too low about yourself," Joe remarked.

"But it is the truth. I have not really written…"

"It doesn't matter. The editorial team were impressed with your book, Sarah. They loved every bit of it. Most really good writers suck at writing great endings, but you pulled that off. Even my father wants to see you in six weeks," Joe said seriously.

"You've got to be kidding me. Tell me this is a joke," I retorted, mingling with an intense palpitation.

"If this is a joke, I wouldn't have bothered coming here. I know you might think that I've influenced the acceptance of your book, but that is not the case. You are a really fine writer, and you have your own voice."

Tears gathered my eyes slightly. I raised my hand up to my mouth and bit hard on it.

"You are really serious? My book has been accepted?"

"We'll be sending the contract after your meeting with my father. The editorial team wants you to take an active part in the editing because of the language you introduced in your book," Joe said, taking a look at his timepiece.

"I have a plane to catch in an hour," Joe said, taking a gulp of Champagne.

He dipped his hand in his pocket and brought out his card.

"You are my guest, Joe. You don't have to pay for a drink," Michelle said excitedly.

"Are you sure?"

"Yeah. Come on. You brought us really good news. Let's luxuriate in it," Michelle said, picking up her glass. "To a great and successful career for Sarah," she said.

We clinked glasses.

After taking a sip from my glass, I left another bite on my arm, struggling to accept this current reality.

"I'll be in touch in a week Sarah. I'm so proud of you and I'm glad that I was right about you," Joe added, standing up from his chair.

I stood up quickly and embraced him tightly.

"Thank you. Thank you so much," I said.

"You've earned this. I'm a big fan."

After pulling away from Joe, I met Michelle on her feet. I smiled and sniffled at the same time, hindering the impulse to succumb to tears.

I embraced Michelle, leaving a kiss on her cheek.

"You are my angel," I whispered in her ear.

"Alright ladies. I have to leave now."

"I want you to come to my parents' fortieth marriage anniversary," Michelle said, turning to Joe.

"When is that?" Joe asked.

"In four weeks. Sunday."

"I'll come if Sarah agrees to be my date on that day," Joe said, winking at me. I was surprised by this move and oscillated my eyes between Michelle and Joe.

"I think I can handle a date with you," I responded.

"Great. Keep me informed," Joe said as he walked away from the restaurant.

Michelle and I watched him excitedly. I let out a little scream as I hugged her again, attracting the attention of the folks in the restaurant.

I didn't mind the attention. At this point, I couldn't afford to be embarrassed for expressing delight.

"I told you, didn't I?" Michelle asked, taking a bite from her food.

"I didn't really think they would accept it so easily. I was willing to take any harsh criticism."

"You underestimate your work ethics, but that's okay. Winners are like that at times."

I enjoyed the food, but I visualized the impending popularity I could acquire if my book aligned with the preferences of the market.

I didn't think I was imbued with the pride and idiosyncrasies that defined most reputable and popular writers. And for a little while, I wondered whether everything was happening too quickly.

"The devil certainly wears high heels," Michelle whispered, impelling me to look towards the door of the restaurant.

I met Linda and Edmond. They were both looking towards our table. Linda curled her arm around Edmond's waist and left a kiss on his cheek as they walked to a table.

Linda dropped down in a chair and had to force Edmond to sit down by pulling his arm.

Edmond sat down but kept his eyes off our table.

Linda gently placed one hand on his chin and pulled his face towards her.

She spoke in a hushed tone and pointed her finger at his face. Edmond shook his head and sat back in his chair.

"You are staring too much," Michelle said, tapping my shoulder.

I turned back to my food and tried to continue eating. Seeing Edmond again reminded me of our bitter separation and sucked out most of the joy I had mingled with.

"You have done great for yourself. Remain focused."

I managed a smile at Michelle and went back to eating my food. Intermittently, I swiveled at them.

At one point, Linda looked at me, smirking and giggling. I could see Edmond trying to caution her without causing a scene.

Somehow, I derived a bit of joy from Edmond's behavior and felt bad about it soon after. It was frustrating to discover that I hadn't tamed the part of me that was pliable to his exhibitions.

Against Michelle's advice, I kept turning towards their table. Linda attempted to feed Edmond, who refused and drank from his glass of wine instead.

I could see that their relationship wasn't as peaceful as Linda had tried to project. It made me start to wonder if Linda had truly blackmailed him into breaking up with me.

"What if Linda is forcing him to be with her?" I muttered, and cupped my hand over my mouth after realizing that I hadn't said it in my mind.

"You are still thinking about him, aren't you? After everything he has done to you?"

"I think there is more to this. I feel Edmond is not doing this because he wants to."

"That should not bother you anymore. The most important thing is that he decided to make this move. He decided to choose her instead of you. The sooner you accept that, the better."

Michelle's tone was harsh, but she was able to keep her voice down. She exhaled loudly, clearly frustrated by my dangerous attachment to Edmond.

"Have you ever felt this way? My head says I should move on, but my feelings say he needs my help."

"Of course your feelings will say that. What else do you expect? You love him. But if you must move on, you need to start listening to your head."

"I think we should leave. I'm not comfortable with him and Linda around."

Michelle pressed her lips together until they disappeared. She had a glare in her eyes as she looked towards their table.

"I don't like the fact that this is happening to you. You shouldn't be the one feeling uncomfortable. You've already suffered too much."

"I am alright," I said, feigning a smile.

"No, you are not. We are supposed to be celebrating your big news but they've ruined it."

"We can do that someplace else," I insisted.

"Alright then. Let's leave."

Michelle stood at my side, blocking my view of Edmond and Linda. I managed to keep my face forward without turning towards their table.

In Michelle's Cadillac, I felt better. It seemed like I had walked out of a stuffy room and into a ventilated one.

"Where should we go?" Michelle asked.

"We should go to my apartment. I'll make you pasta. My pasta is soo nice."

Michelle's blue eyes blinked excitedly. I was happy to capture the restoration of the excitement that gripped her before the appearance of Edmond and Linda.

Michelle turned on the stereo, nodding her head to the song blaring out from the speaker.

After a little while, my phone beeped. I picked it up and found that it was Edmond. I turned to Michelle. She hadn't noticed.

Quickly I unlocked my phone and read through the message:

You are so beautiful and I'm really glad that you've remained beautiful after everything I have done to you. I hope the future is better. I hope I can still do something about it.

"What are you reading?" Michelle asked suddenly.

"Oh! Nothing. I was just browsing," I said smiling theatrically.

XXIII

EDMOND

I sat beside a rock at the prestige beach in Santa Catalina. This was Linda's favorite beach, and she had insisted on spending the weekend here to tighten our bond.

There were a few folks in lounge chairs that overlooked the beach. There were a handful of surfers in the beach, and their sport offered some form of entertainment to me.

Linda was, by far, the hottest at the beach. She wore a red bikini and walked majestically, attracting the attention of some of the men and women.

I was sitting in a lounge chair, uninterested in getting myself wet as I sipped on a coconut.

This was supposed to be fun, but I wanted the weekend to end quickly.

Linda walked into the water and flailed her hands as she waited for the tide. She dropped down on her knees and dipped herself into the water at it gushed towards her.

She was giggling when she got out of the water. She waved at me and started in my direction. She kept responding to waves and cheers, giving off a chummy smile.

"Did you see that?" she asked, sitting in the lounge chair beside me.

"I did. You were clearly having fun."

"Why do you sound moody?" she asked.

"Want some coconut water?" I asked, stretching my coconut towards her.

"No. Tell me why you're moody?"

"I'm not moody. I just don't want to be here."

Linda was miffed by my response. She slapped my shoulder.

"You are so ungrateful. I'm doing this for your legacy," she barked. Her voice was loud. She sounded like a woman scolding her little child.

"Keep your voice down."

"No. I'm not keeping my voice down. Let the whole world know how ungrateful you are," she retorted.

I looked to my side and found some interested ladies and gentlemen. I waved them off.

"You are attracting unnecessary attention."

"I don't fucking care. You really wanted to replace me with Sarah. That was so disrespectful."

I couldn't believe that Linda had suddenly decided to confront me in the presence of everyone.

"Let's talk about this in the room," I said pleadingly in a hushed tone.

"No. Answer me right here."

I tried to stand up from my chair, but her hand tightened around the lapel of my short-sleeved shirt.

"Where do you think you're going?"

I took a deep breath, resisting the impulse to stave into anger. I knew I would be blamed if things got out of hand. It would be difficult to blame a beautiful lady in this kind of situation.

"You forced your way back into my life. This is not about my legacy. This is about you and your family blackmailing me with my family's legacy."

Linda loosened her hands from my shirt and frowned at me.

"What happened to you? You used to be sweet to me. You used to love me like there's nothing else in the world you'd rather love."

"And you don't know what changed, do you? You cheated on me and it wasn't the first time. You kept doing it until I caught you."

"Why do you always bring up the past whenever I'm trying to solve our issues?"

"It's not just the past for me, Linda. It is the reality. I don't think I'll ever see you the same way."

I stood up from the lounge chair without any form of interruption from Linda, who looked cold and thoughtful.

Moments later, I was in the hallway leading to our hotel room. I stopped beside the door of our hotel room and thought about abandoning the plans to remain here until Sunday.

Induced by this thought, I went inside and started packing my clothes into my luggage.

Linda came into the room with a fierce, angry expression.

"What do you think you're doing?" she asked.

"This is not going to work. This vacation will only make things worse."

"No. It has to work and it's going to work," she said, charging towards me. "You were going to abandon me? You were going to leave me here alone?"

"You know I don't want you. Why can't you just accept that?"

"I'm not going to listen to anything you say right now. You're clearly not alright upstairs. You love me, Ed. You wrote me so many poems. That's the Ed I believe."

"That Ed is dead."

"No. He's right here," she said, punching my chest lightly. "You are going to give him to me."

"You can find someone else. You're beautiful. You're young."

"Shut up," Linda said, breathing heavily. "I can't lose you. I won't lose you. I won't lose you to that bitch."

"She is not a bitch! Don't talk about her lik…"

Linda landed a heavy slap on my face before I could complete my statement. Her eyes were dilated and her breathing was raspy.

"How dare you praise her in front of me."

"You slapped me?!"

Linda exhaled loudly and reeled back. She sniffled and broke down in tears. It was an unexpected, mechanistic move that changed the dimension of the situation before us.

She bawled loudly, but her eyes didn't look like they were tinged with sadness.

I was afraid of this version of Linda. It was a side that I didn't really notice during my first spell with her.

"It's your fault," she said, snuffling. "You insult me. You treat me like trash."

My right hand was still placed on the part of my face she had slapped.

For a while, I vacillated my eyes between her and my luggage.

I grabbed my luggage and rolled it forward.

"Don't fuck with me Ed! My father will never see me cry. He'll do everything to ruin your company. He'll do anything for me. Don't mess with me."

I turned to Linda and discovered that she had stopped crying. She had wiped her eyes and wore the expression she had taken before landing a slap on my face.

"This relationship has to work! I can't live with myself if you marry someone else," she said, moving towards me.

Linda's hands were shaking and she walked gingerly. She looked like she was struck by an amalgam of fear, anger, and desperation.

She placed her hands on my cheek and kicked the luggage at my side. Linda was inured to the pain from kicking the luggage. She looked high and her hands quivered as she placed them on my cheeks.

Her eyes were firm, unblinking, and coated with insanity. She was unstable and her condition seemed to worsen with every passing day.

"You have to be with me. You must be with me," she declared.

Her hands continued to shake, leaving me short of words. I almost started to feel sorry for her.

"Say something, Honey. Tell me you love me. Tell me you love me so much," she said, leaning closer. Her eyes were full of pain at this point. She looked like a baby that was begging to be held by its parents.

I opened my mouth and closed it back. I was still speechless.

She sniffled and exhaled deeply. Her lips were inches away from mine.

"I know you can see that I love you. It's so obvious. It's so fucking obvious," she bawled as she took her hands from my cheek.

She picked up the luggage at my side and took it back to the wardrobe, hurling it inside.

She turned back to me and took off her bikini bra, revealing her perky, firm breasts. She always resorted to sex because she knew it was my weak spot.

She walked slowly toward me, rubbing her breast against my chest.

"You enjoy it, don't you? You enjoy me so much. You've told me several times in the past. I need that Ed back. I'll do anything to get that Ed back."

She drew her lips closer and kissed me. I took two steps backward.

"I don't feel that way anymore. You really need to get used to this fact. I think it'll make us better."

"No. This is the devil's work. We are meant to be together. Remember when we wrote our names in the sand and waited for the tide to wash them off?"

"This will not help, Linda. Marriage is a lifetime commitment. Why do you want to spend it with a man that doesn't love you anymore?"

"You love me. You've always loved me. This is just a setback."

Linda closed in on me, wrapping her arms around my neck, forcing me to recline against the wall behind me.

"I don't think I can stay in this room. I have to leave," I said.

"Why can't you ever be grateful Ed? Do you know how many people would dream to be in this position? Didn't you see the other men making passes at me? They love my body, but I want it to belong to only you."

She kissed me, forcefully, moving her hand towards my shorts. I grabbed her hand, and held on tightly to it, ensuring she couldn't reach my penis.

"What's wrong with you? Let me make love to you. Please let me make love to you."

She pressed her lips against mine, but I quickly turned my face to the side.

"We have to leave."

"If you leave, there will be consequences."

"I have heard that several times."

"You don't want to be accused of murder."

"What?"

"I could kill myself and make sure you're held responsible. I know how I'd achieve that. And I don't even have to kill myself. I could really harm myself and make you the scape goat."

"You are not yourself, Linda. This is becoming crazy."

"I'm crazy for you. You drive me crazy every single day, Ed. You think Sarah can love you like I do? You think she will be willing to die for you?"

"This is not love, Linda. This is insanity."

"What's the difference. I need you and I'm willing to do everything. Everything," she said, restoring the position of her hands on my cheeks.

"Let me kiss you. Please don't fight me," she said breathing heavily. She sucked on my bottom lip, unbothered by my lack of responsiveness.

Slowly, she unbuttoned my shirt, and flung it away. She dipped her hand in my shorts, taking advantage of the moment.

As she grabbed my penis, I started to think that I might not really be choosing my family's legacy by deciding to be with her. It started to feel like I was choosing death and oblivion. I was choosing misery and a life of constant regret.

"I love you so much. I want only you, Ed. Only you," she said, and started another round of steamy kissing.

She grabbed my hand and placed it on her back.

I didn't try to fight her moves. I was afraid Linda could really do the things she had told me. There was an eerie coldness I found in her eyes.

She turned me around, applying her weight on my body as she forced me to back away to the bed.

Her right hand was inside my shorts. Unfortunately, my penis didn't care about the current trajectory of my mind. It couldn't shake off Linda's enchantment.

She pushed me and smiled as I landed in the bed. She jumped into the bed and kept my body between her legs as she knelt before me.

"You want this, Ed. Your body wants this. Stop fighting it. I'm the one your body desires. I am the one that rocks your world," she said, dragging my shorts from my waist.

"Now look at that," she said, rolling her tongue around her top lip. "You're so big."

She pressed her hands on my neck and initiated another round of kissing as she choked me. Her breathing was heavy and her kisses were intense.

I was relaxed, losing the fight in me. I knew I couldn't afford to leave her alone in this hotel. Linda's desperation was a real concern because she created the impression that she had nothing else to live for.

XXIV
EDMOND

The vacation with Linda felt like a sentence, and freedom only came on the ride back to Pomona.

Linda was excited and kept making videos on Snapchat. Her smile and giggles were beautiful. The Mona Lisa portrait she painted for the world was full of color and life, yet our reality felt like I was living beneath a dark cloud that was ready to gush forth rain.

We reached my father's mansion in the evening. Linda comported herself, giving off a demureness that most older women would be proud of.

She wore a gray hat and long black dress that reached her ankles. She curled one arm around the crook of my elbow.

We looked like a happy couple without a single problem in our relationship. Linda kissed my cheek in the doorway and giggled. Her energy intensified my fear for our future.

Linda looked to have cultivated the skills to make compelling public appearances, which, I felt, made her a danger to my welfare. I couldn't think of a way I could leave her without being the antagonist in our tale.

On the ground floor, I met Evans and his wife. They were already in a meeting with my parents. The aura was cheerful and it looked like both families had finally accepted the impending alignment of the future of their children.

My mother stood up from her chair and walked towards us. She embraced us together, and Linda kissed her cheek.

"You guys look so happy," my mom said.

"Ed was great and really lively. I enjoyed my time with him," Linda said, embracing me.

I couldn't believe the lies.

My mother accompanied us to the living room where we exchanged pleasantries and basked theatrically in our unfortunate time together.

Surprisingly, Linda had photographic evidence of these moments and a believable smile on her face. She was a great actress and tucked herself between Mr. Evans and my father, who sat together on a couch.

Mr. Evans kept smiling and followed the exciting stories of Linda. I was shocked by the level of mendacity she employed in her tales. Most of these encounters were products of her imagination and the few experiences captured in photos were as a result of her forceful charges and manipulations.

We both knew the vacation was a nightmare, but Linda expressed her ability to turn a nightmare into a lovely, beautiful story.

"I didn't know Ed was so romantic," Evans said, smiling at me. I returned his smile halfheartedly.

My father kept a smile on his face, but I had a feeling he knew Linda's stories weren't entirely true.

Linda stood up from between them and came to me. She sat on my lap and kissed my lips.

"Get a room," Mrs. Evans said, casting a blushed smile.

"My husband," Linda said, leaving another kiss on my lips.

She was all over me, and I couldn't show any form of revulsion in the presence of her parents.

"Your father and I were just talking about an important business," Evans said, seriously, fixing his eyes on me.

"What is it father?" Linda asked.

"We are planning your marriage to Ed. We want it to be grand. This is important for our families. Isn't that so Mr. Barker?" Evans asked.

"Yeah. The future is bright for both of our families and it's really great to see that you two are really in love."

"Awwn," Linda said, leaving a kiss on my lips.

"What destination do you guys prefer?" Evans asked. "I was thing about Texas. Mr. Barker thinks Colorado would be great."

Linda turned towards me and giggled.

"Why can't we hold it in LA?" Linda asked.

"Is that what you want?" Evans asked.

"I don't know. I just want it to be beautiful," Linda responded.

"What do you think, Ed?" Evans asked.

"Texas sounds great. I had a great time the last time I was there," I replied.

"See?" Evans asked, turning to my father. "Your son has the same taste as me."

Evans took a sip of whiskey and raised up his glass.

"I hope your eventual marriage brings beauty and joy to both our families," Evans said.

Everyone else raised a glass apart from Linda and me. Linda kissed me as our family clinked glasses.

Moments later, Linda took my hand as we accompanied her parents to their Porsche.

"I thought you were going to leave with them," I said softly.

"No. I don't want to get my eyes off you. I want to be by your side all the time."

"Why?"

"Because I love you," she said, leaving a kiss on my cheek before my parents.

She walked with me to my duplex and slouched against the door after closing it.

"See? You didn't do bad at all back there. We can do this, Ed. We can really do this."

I didn't know how to respond to her statement. Linda walked from the door and dropped her hands on my shoulder.

"No one can conquer a man trying to do his best. Do your best. We'll have a beautiful marriage."

"I think you should go back home Linda. I think we'll both benefit from not being in each other's faces all the time."

"No. I'm not leaving you. I don't trust you."

"What do you mean?"

"I know you'll try to go back to her. That's what you've always wanted to do."

"So why do you keep fighting?"

"Because I love you! I made a mistake… Why can't you just forgive me?" Linda responded.

"You are not even the woman I loved, Linda. I loved something that didn't exist," I said walking towards the stairs.

"You can say whatever you want, Ed. You can try to make me feel bad for loving you, but I'm not leaving. I'm stuck with you for life."

I stopped at the stairs and turned around. Linda was breathing heavily and had a glare in her eyes as she looked up at me. I turned around and walked up the stairs, unwilling to be involved in another episode of her madness.

XXV

SARAH

The receptionist stepped into my office with a bouquet of tulips. She wore glasses and held out the bouquet as she walked to my desk.

"This came for you," she said, handing me the bouquet.

"Thank you," I responded, slightly conflicted. I didn't think there was anyone out there that would send me flowers, but I knew who I wanted them to be from.

I waited for the receptionist to leave my office before I took out the card attached to the flower:

I hope you receive flowers from time-to-time Sarah. You are beautiful both in words and appearance, and I can only see a great future for you.

Sincerely,

Joe Benny.

This message brightened my morning and showed how Joe preferred to speak in a language of romance. It was nice to get some attention again too.

I sniffed the bouquet, appeased by its beautiful, sweet smell. It was the first time I would be receiving flowers since I started working in Hutchinson & Co Legal. To be fair, it was the first time I had received flowers in my life.

I picked up the bouquet and stood up from my chair. I walked to the window and sniffed the bouquet as I looked towards the road.

I didn't try to confuse Joe's gesture with a romantic, sexual move. I knew it was borne out of admiration because he had indicated from the start that he wasn't sexually interested in me.

Moments later, I was on my way to Michelle's office. I wanted to share the good news with her.

I hummed a song in the hallway, taking frequent sniffs at the bouquet.

I heard the sound of whispering voices from Michelle's office. The door was slightly ajar, and I was able to take a peep. It was Michelle and her father.

"I think Mr. Evans intends to betray my plans with him," Hutchinson said concernedly.

"I thought the agreement was already sealed," Michelle responded.

"Not really. I think Evans wants to double-cross us. Steward has not received any signal from him."

"What does this mean?" Michelle asked.

"I think it has to do with his daughter. You see, Linda is getting married to Edmond. I think Evans wants to keep the investment in his family."

"That is actually a good motive father."

"But it hadn't always been so Michelle. Evans doesn't even like Mr. Barker. I think there's more to this. I think he's using everyone."

"What do we do?"

"I don't know. Steward says he would pull out of the deal if Evans doesn't get back to him in a month."

"So what happens to you and your interest?"

"That's the problem. I'll have to start from scratch. Maybe I'll just abandon my interest in the real estate sector."

"Doesn't Steward have an alternative plan?"

"Steward only has fifty one percent of his company share. He's struggling to retain control. We only have a chance with Barker's shareholders because they're so many that hold small shares."

"Then let's do it without Evans."

"Evans already has an agreement in place. That is the problem. He is a great negotiator."

"Don't think too much its father. We're doing quite well with our other investments."

"Yeah. But growth has to be a continuous process."

I stepped away from the door, overwhelmed by the information I had received.

I hurried back to my office and dropped the bouquet on my desk. I was troubled by the reality of Edmond's impending marriage to Linda. This new information seemed to shatter the little part of me that believed that I still had a chance with him.

Apart from that afternoon in Michelle's Cadillac, Edmond had sent me other messages, complimenting my beauty and attitude, but I had managed to stave off the impulse to respond to his texts.

I sat back in my chair, thoughtful and curious. It took some time before I was able to process and make sense of the information I had received.

Incidentally, a knock came on my office door. Michelle stepped inside and closed the door.

Her eyes were pinned on the bouquet on my desk.

"Hmm. You have a new admirer?" she asked, slouching against my office desk.

"This came from Joe."

"Joe? That's strange. I thought he was supposed to be in New York."

"Yeah. I think he sent someone to deliver them."

"Hmm. That's very thoughtful. Has he been making passes at you?"

"Passes? No."

"Well, he wouldn't come to my parents' anniversary unless you agreed to be his date. I think he likes you."

"Maybe, but I don't think it has anything to do with romance."

"Why would you think so? Joe is very romantic and he's a decent guy as well."

"Well, he told me he's not sexually attracted to me."

"He did?" Michelle asked, drooping down on my desk.

I nodded, picked up the bouquet, and sniffed on it.

"I think you should keep your mind open. He may have changed his mind."

"I don't think I'm ready for any relationship. Besides, Edmond said there are rumors that Joe could be gay."

"Really? I haven't heard any such rumors. Joe is a confident guy. If he's gay, I think his loved ones would know."

I took a long sniff at the bouquet and dropped it on the table. I sat back and took a deep breath. Michelle was texting away on her phone and smiling.

"I would need the Lincoln LLC contract on Thursday. I hope you can get it ready by then?" Michelle asked, looking up from her phone.

"We are already working on it. I'm supervising it myself."

"Great," Michelle said, turning back to her phone. As she typed on her phone, I thought about the information I had received from her office door.

"Edmond always said there was so much at stake," I said, thoughtfully. Michelle raised her face up from her phone and squinted her eyes.

"I can't believe you are bringing him up. He's getting married to Linda soon. When are you going to give up?"

"He is going to marry her against his will. I overheard you and your father."

"What does that have to do with anything?"

"Edmond said there's so much at stake. I think what's at stake is the agreement Evans has with the shareholders of his father's company."

Michelle stood up from the table and pressed her lips together. I was relieved to see that she was actually thinking about my suggestion. In the silence that came between us, Michelle backed away and sat on the chair at the end of my office.

"I think you might have a point. Edmond hasn't always been like this," Michelle said, thoughtfully.

"Exactly. I think he's being blackmailed, and he doesn't want to talk about it to give their families bad publicity," I insisted.

"This is interesting, Sarah, but there's hardly anything we can do about it. In fact, you have to keep this information to yourself. You don't want to get in trouble for this."

"What if Edmond needs help? What if he's simply giving me a hint?"

"What hint? He broke up with you because he couldn't help himself. Besides, if he wanted your help, he would have told you about his situation."

"He is still texting me," I responded, glibly.

Michelle stood up from her chair and leaned against my desk. She shook her head.

"And you didn't tell me about it?"

"I... I... You wouldn't really understand how I feel. I just thought you'd be disappointed with me."

Michelle was quiet and had a thoughtful look. She turned towards the window at the side as she leaned against my desk.

I felt guilty. I didn't want to be on her bad side and Michelle's protracted silence became a real concern for me.

I stood up from my chair, disconsolate as I watched her.

"I'm so sorry. Please say something."

Michelle turned to me and stood upright.

"You should have told me about it, but to be fair, you didn't have to."

"Don't say that. I was overthinking your response. And I shouldn't have done that. You are the only reason why I still have my head up."

"Does he say he wants to get back with you?"

"He has mostly been vague, but I've not been responding to his texts. I don't think I should.

Michelle folded her hands across her stomach and moved towards me.

"I can see you really love him, but you have to stop taking his texts once he gets married to Linda. You have to make it clear that he shouldn't try to reach you anymore."

Michelle placed one hand on my shoulder.

"I have to leave now. I have some work to do."

"Are you mad at me for not telling you about his texts?" I asked quickly.

"I was a bit disappointed, but I totally understand. Sometimes people seek healing from the people that hurt them."

"Is that what it is? You really think I'm finding healing from his text?" I asked.

"You know he's miserable as well. I think that gives you some form of comfort. You know you're not the only one suffering."

"I think you may have a point."

"I know because after breaking up with my ex, I watched him. I wanted to see if he would feel miserable. When I found out that it was easy for him to move on, I was heartbroken. It is heartbreaking to be miserable alone," Michelle said, smiling sadly.

Michelle walked away, keeping her face down. She stopped in the doorway and turned to me.

"Don't give up until you're absolutely sure it can no longer work between you two," Michelle said, and walked out of my office.

The sadness in her voice brought tears to my eyes. My breathing became heavy and my mind descended into an inordinate rampage of accommodating several diverse voices.

I walked to the door and took a look across the hallway. It was empty. Michelle's parting statement made me wonder whether I needed to go to her office to keep her company.

I walked back to my desk, picked up the bouquet and sniffed it. I took out the card and reread the message. Although I found Joe's message beautiful, I didn't think I was ready to accommodate a change in the relationship I had with him.

I thought it was unfortunate that my life could be infused in permanent damage if Edmond eventually married Linda. Although I had only known him for a short while, I struggled to imagine my life with someone else. What was it about him that made my heart helplessly attached to him?

I sat back in my chair for a while and entertained the messages I had received from Edmond since meeting him in Settlers.

I sat up and turned on my laptop. Work was the only worthwhile distraction for the tormenting memory of lost love.

Gradually, I became immersed in my work. I worked on a partnership deed, proofreading and incorporating the relevant terminologies for the contract.

My phone beeped. It was a soft, low beep, but it was enough to take my attention from my laptop.

After opening my phone, I found Edmond's message. I was eerily stricken by the rush of guilt I felt during Michelle's protracted silence. I wondered whether the time had come for me to respond to Edmond's message.

I thumbed my phone and sat back:

Hey, Sarah. It's me again. The thorn in your heart. I wish I was in your shoes. At least I would be able to understand the depth of your pain. I wish I could take all the pain you feel from my silence and lack of direction. I am still as guilty as the very first day. If this is the end, I want you to know that I can never stop loving you. I would always remember the love life that I couldn't live.

I started to type a reply to his message. It was supposed to be about my decision to move on from him, but as his text continued to echo through my mind, it eventually gripped me. Edmond was just as miserable as I am.

I deleted the message I had typed and dropped my phone. At this point, silence remained the most sensible response.

XXVI
SARAH

This was going to be a beautiful day. I knew it as soon as I woke up in the morning. It flashed in my mind as I looked in the mirror, preparing for Michelle's parents' marriage anniversary.

I had chosen a white dress this time. It had a high slit and an extra layer of pleated silver-colored material looped down from the back. I had chosen silver-colored shoes and bag, and it took me a long time to decide on the right wristwatch.

Eventually, I went for the silver wristwatch I had received from Edmond because it was beautiful and gelled with my outfit. At least that was what I thought, but I kept staring at it, receiving flashes of the memory that brought it to me.

I intended to wait inside my apartment until I received Joe's call or message.

It was a short wait, but it felt long. I mingled with thoughts that occupied every moment that I waited.

From the ongoing plans, there were indications that Edmond's marriage to Sarah was just a month away.

It was a painful realization. And at the moment, I thought that the world was a place where evil was meant to thrive. My experiences had pushed me towards having approximate perceptions with Michelle.

The world had no room for fairytales. It frowned at it and reminded us that pain was its greatest essence.

These thoughts didn't feel like they belonged to my body, but my body hadn't felt like it belonged to me since I lost Edmond.

Love was supposed to be life's greatest essence, and I was supposed to find it in the people I was huddled up with. I was supposed to find beauty in this world through the lovely exhibitions of others. These thoughts didn't feel like they belonged to a woman that woke up, looking forward to an auspicious day.

I walked in front of the mirror and placed my hands on my waist.

"I'm beautiful and beautiful things will always find me," I said, halfheartedly. I kept repeating these words and moved around the living room.

Moments later, I was screaming them out loud like a lunatic that had finally made peace with madness.

I was breathing heavily when I stopped screaming. I felt a headachy sensation tapping away at the back of my head.

I went to the kitchen and drank water. Internally, I kept saying those words. They eventually felt like they came from my soul. It felt like it was my spirit's way of reminding me that nights would not last forever.

My story with Edmond might be closing in on its end, but these words wanted me to believe that another chapter would open soon. Perhaps it would be with someone even more beautiful. Perhaps life had one more twist in my tale.

It was when I walked out of the kitchen that my phone started to ring. It was Joe.

Coincidence?

"Hello," I said.

"I'm downstairs babe," he responded.

I turned to the wall clock. The time was 7:37pm. He had come early.

"I'll be right down," I said, and hung up.

Slow and steady, I walked. I kept my head straight. I kept miserable thoughts from my mind. I thought about the tulips from Joe. I thought about Michelle's benevolence at Top Luxury. These were landmarks. Landmarks of joy.

Outside the elevator lobby, I saw a limo. Joe had chosen a grey suit for the party. It was the first time I had seen him in dull colors, and he looked great in the suit.

He was holding a bouquet of pink roses in one hand, and the smile on his face broadened as he walked towards me.

"You're as beautiful as ever," he said, and handed me the bouquet. He leaned closer and left a kiss on my cheek. It was a beautiful kiss.

I was smiling. I felt like a princess. He weaved his arm around the crook of my elbow and opened the back door.

I climbed inside and found a big smile on his face before he closed the door.

He joined me from the other side and sat up.

"You are beautiful. You should visit the hospital sometimes. There are lots of people's faces that would light up just by looking at how beautiful you are."

"Joe. Why are always so kind to me?"

"I wish I was struggling to say these things, but I'm not. Some people just have that spark in their eyes. Some people get their spark from the love of others."

"I'm not sure I understand you."

"You look like you can shine on your own, Sarah. Your heart has not been corrupted by the greed and wickedness in this world."

"Why do you think so? I have pains as well. I have learnt that love can make one miserable. I have started to feel drained and incapable of loving again."

"And yet you love. You open your heart to this world. You are in pain and yet you are able to smile so beautifully. That's your spark. I think you see beauty before material things."

"You don't really know me, Joe. You have been great to me. I have been fascinated by your energy, but I'm not sure your admiration is based on knowledge."

Joe smiled and pushed up tendrils of hair from his brow.

"I know why you think this way. You don't see me around. And you think the first time I met you was at my father's birthday."

"That was not the first time?" I asked, surprised.

"No. It was only the first time I spoke to you."

"Have you been stalking me?"

"No, but I've noticed you. I've seen what you bring in your friendship with Michelle."

I couldn't take my eyes off Joe and the implication of his statement.

"Is there something you're not telling me?" I asked.

"Maybe."

"You said you're not sexually attracted to me the first time I saw you. I hope that has not changed."

"It hasn't changed."

"I'm not sure there's another man in this world that would treat a lady this way without wanting to have romantic dealings."

"Romantic dealings," Joe said, smiling. "I like the sound of that word, but romance isn't necessarily sexual."

"What is it that you haven't told me? Are you gay?"

Joe looked confused, took a deep breath, and sat back in his chair.

"I'm sorry. I shouldn't have asked that question."

"It is okay. Really, it's alright."

"Are you sure?"

"Yeah."

I turned to the bouquet and sniffed it. I didn't think Joe was comfortable with my question and wished I could take it back.

"I take back my question. I'm so sorry."

"Don't apologize," Joe said, smiling. "A question is a question. Maybe it's borne out of suspicion, but it's still a question."

Joe was still looking towards me, gauging the expression on my face.

The limo pulled up outside the Hutchinson mansion. I noticed that Joe was still looking in my direction.

I was unnerved by the look in his eyes and the silence that punctuated this exchange. I thought he was deliberating on revealing his feelings for me. The signs had always been there, and it scared me that I was going to be put in a position where I would need to make a decision on his feelings for me.

"We are here," I said, in a hushed tone, breaking the silence between us.

"Yeah. You're right," he said, and took a deep breath.

He stepped out of the car and moved to my side. He opened the door and took my hand.

We walked together, slowly, and in the same stride. With Joe by my side, I lost the usual impulse to look around my environment. His presence was enough. His eyes regarded me like they were willing to worship me.

I felt bigger beside him. I felt protected and only beautiful thoughts ran across my mind.

He took my hand as we walked into the banquet room. The sound of music pervaded the floor.

Hutchinson and his wife were at the door, welcoming the guests.

The banquet had been rearranged. There were tables and cushioned chairs and it looked like Hutchinson had, as expected, kept attendance strictly based on invitation.

A steward walked us to our table. There were four adjoined chairs to our table.

Joe pulled out a chair and waited for me to sit down.

"There is a card in the bouquet. Don't you want to read it?" Joe asked. I smiled and took out the card.

I know you'll look beautiful today even if you don't try so much. It's in your nature to be beautiful. It's in your nature to bring beauty into the lives of those around you.

I looked up at him, unsure whether I should be delighted or afraid.

"I don't even know what to say anymore. You always know how to find the right words. It should be a crime to have the ability to say so many beautiful things in one day," I said, rereading his message.

Michelle came to our table while my eyes were on the card. She tapped my shoulder, jerking me off the mesmerism sprinkled in Joe's text.

"You look so beautiful," I said, looking up at her.

Michelle's blonde hair cascaded freely down to the nape of her neck, and there were genuine scrims of happiness in her blue eyes.

I stood up and embraced her. Michelle held on tightly to me. It was an awkward embrace. It felt like I was the celebrant.

"I am so happy to see you Sarah."

"We spoke last night," I replied.

"Yeah. But so much can change in a day."

Michelle's eyes blinked repeatedly. She looked like she was holding back the impulse to surrender to tears. She inhaled deeply and turned to Joe, who was already on his feet.

"I'm happy to see you. Your energy is intoxicating," Michelle said, embracing him.

I could see Joe's eyes as Michelle embraced him. They were puppy-eyed, like a child reunited with his mom after spending time in daycare.

When they parted, Joe held on to Michelle's hand.

"You are so beautiful today," he complimented.

"Thank you," Michelle responded, and walked away from our table.

Joe looked over his shoulder at Michelle. He watched her as she went to her parents.

"Joe," I whispered. Joe turned to me. The look in his eyes hadn't changed a bit.

He sat down and reached for the bottle of wine on our table. He opened it and filled his glass halfway. He picked up another glass and filled it halfway.

"What are you thinking about?" I asked.

"Nothing."

"It doesn't feel that way."

"Well, feelings aren't always reality," he responded, and handed the other glass to me.

"There is something you want to tell me, Joe. Why not say it?"

"So you've figured me out finally?"

"Tell me."

"Why do I have a feeling you already know," he said, taking a sip of wine.

"You didn't observe me because you wanted me, did you? You were observing someone else."

Joe smiled and looked into his glass as if something had fallen inside. It was perhaps his tears because his eyes were wet and glinted.

He opened his mouth and kept it open. It was the first time I had seen the usually confident Joe short of words. His lips quivered as he kept his mouth open. The words wouldn't come out because his memories and thoughts had become vivid, like stars in a clear blue sky.

"Joe," I called. He closed his mouth and took another sip of wine.

"She was miserable Sarah. Her last relationship broke her. I knew he wasn't genuine, but I didn't know he loved her so much."

"What are you talking about?" I asked. At this point, I was more confused than ever.

"I have always loved her, but if she's not going to be with me, she deserves to be with someone that adores her."

"Who are you talking about?"

"I made plans. I set him up. I sent anonymous messages to Michelle informing her that he was in a hotel with another girl. He was wasting the money she had sent him for business."

"Joe."

"Yes."

"You love Michelle?"

"She became better when you came into the picture. Her sockets were not always swollen anymore. I couldn't be more grateful for what you've done for her. You are the friend she always needed."

Joe took a gulp and smiled at me. He looked better, but I was still in shock. Until his embrace with Michelle, there had been no sign of his feelings for her.

"I don't get it. Why haven't you tried to be in her life? Why haven't you tried to pursue her?"

"I have always been in her life, but I've learnt to keep my distance."

"But why would you want to stay away from someone you love?"

"She is broken. She's still healing. Staying away is the most selfless thing to do."

"No. Maybe now is the time for you to be selfish, Joe. You are a great guy. You are the kind of guy that Michelle needs."

"But you don't know me."

"I know your spirit."

"My spirit?"

"Yes. How do you not see that you're the kind of blessing she needs in this world?"

As Joe opened his mouth to say something, Michelle came to our table and tapped Joe's shoulder.

"Let's take a picture," she said, taking his hand. With her other hand, she grabbed my hand.

She squeezed herself between us. There was a photographer before us. He leaned down and took quick snapshots.

I passed the photographer my phone and he took a couple more photos on my phone.

As I pulled away from Michelle, willed to find any chemistry between her and Joe, Joe was still standing close to her. He had taken that look that revealed his feelings for her.

I took my phone back from the photographer and scrolled through the photos taken of us. Joe and Michelle looked great together. From their outfits, to the color of their eyes, they really complimented each other.

"I hope you're making yourself comfortable?" Michelle asked.

"Yeah. Sarah's presence has been comforting," Joe responded.

"You two are developing a great chemistry," Michelle said, and looked towards the top of the room. "I have to join my father," she added, and walked away.

I followed Joe's eyes as he looked at her.

"Please say something before the end of the party. If you don't, I'll tell her myself."

Joe looked away from Michelle, shaken slightly by my words. His lips trembled before he sat back in his chair.

"Don't do that, Sarah. Please don't."

"I won't if you tell her tonight."

"Don't speak on my behalf. If the time comes when I have to tell her, I'll tell her myself."

Joe was looking away from me as he spoke. His eyes were at the overhung platform at the top of the floor.

"Remaining quiet is the only way you can really respect me," Joe added.

Hutchinson's speech was beautiful. It was focused on his wife and the beautiful moments that defined their love.

I was thinking about Joe's feelings for Michelle. I was afraid he wouldn't find the right time to divulge his feelings for her. Perhaps looking for the right time was his greatest impediment.

I looked around the room, left, right, and just as I intended to turn back to Joe, I met Linda.

Her eyes were on me, but she had an expressionless look. It seemed she pondered my relationship with Joe.

I looked to her side and found Edmond. He was looking towards Hutchinson, listening to his speech.

At the end of the speech, a round of applause permeated the room and we stood to our feet. I was delighted that Michelle had a happy family. She had a father that loved her, and it was refreshing to see her smiling so much.

At the end of the speech, we were blessed by music from a gospel singer. Michelle came to our table amidst the rendition. She sat down and placed one hand on my shoulder.

"I am really happy this is going so well," she said, turning to Joe. "Is there something else you want?"

"No. I'm alright. This wine is really good," Joe responded.

I kept oscillating my eyes between Michelle and Joe. I didn't even care so much about my happiness at this moment. I wanted something to happen between them. I wanted Cupid to strike his arrows and ignite their hearts until they were connected.

"I am thinking we should go on a vacation this summer," Michelle said, suddenly, stroking my hair.

"Vacation? That sounds great," I responded.

"I'm sure you'll be really busy," Michelle said, turning to Joe.

"Oh! I can make time for a vacation. But it depends on the location," Joe responded.

"Where would you like to go?" Michelle asked.

"Tuscany," Joe responded.

"Why do I like that idea? I have heard a bit about Florence and maybe I'd consider it," Michelle responded.

"We could go together," I added. "The three of us would have a great time."

Michelle turned to Joe and swiveled back at me.

"I don't know if it's a good idea," Michelle said.

"I think it's a good idea. I love it already," Joe responded.

"Really? Okay then. We'll just plan towards it," Michelle added.

"I'll be in touch," Joe responded.

In that instant, my phone beeped. A comic was on stage, but I hadn't been following his jokes while we conversed.

I took out my phone from my bag and saw a message from Edmond. I turned to Michelle and met her eyes.

I honestly didn't want to read the message. I feared the emotions it would unlock whilst I was in the presence of so many people.

I put my phone back in my bag. Michelle leaned towards me and gave me a hug.

"You'll be alright," she whispered in my ear.

As I turned my head, I met Linda's eyes. She had a frown on her face, but I didn't really care. Edmond was also looking towards me as if to see my reaction to his message.

I turned my face back towards the comic on stage, but from the corner of my eye I could see Edmond stand up and start walking towards our table.

Every step he took left me with intense stabs of palpitations. Although I could see the crowd around me laughing hysterically, the intense drum of my heart drowned out every sound.

Edmonds stood above me and I could see that his eyes were full of sorrow and misery.

He stretched out his hand towards me.

"Sarah, please, can we talk?"

I looked across the room to where Linda was sitting. Her face was filled with embarrassment and anger. She literally looked like she was going to explode.

"Sarah, please, I'm so sorry for everything. I know how much I've hurt you, but I don't care anymore. I don't care about the consequences. I just want to be with you. I can't afford to lose you."

Tears gathered in his eyes and I could see striking sincerity in his gaze.

Linda stormed off from her table, charging towards the exit door. The door slammed behind her which was enough to catch the attention of everyone in the room.

Ed pulled his hand back from me.

"I will die before I leave you again. I'll explain everything. I'll tell you why it was difficult for me to leave her. I promise"

"Please sit down. Please. People are looking at you," I said.

"I don't care. I have hidden you for too long."

"Today is special for Michelle's parents. You should care."

Edmond sat down in the empty chair at my side. Joe was quiet, observant. Michelle kept her hand on my shoulder.

"Well, as I was saying before the brunette got into a hissy fit," the comedian continued, bringing life back to the room.

Edmond grabbed onto my hands and held them in the palm of his as he looked into my eyes. I just wanted to hug him and kiss him and tell him I forgave him for everything, but what was to say he wouldn't leave me again for Linda in a couple of months.

Edmond turned and looked at Joe.

"Are you two a thing now?" Edmond's face became even more upset.

I wanted to lie to him, just to make him a little jealous so that maybe he could understand how I felt every time I saw him with Linda, but before I could Joe let out a little chuckle.

"She's a special woman, and she's truly beautiful both inside and out, but we're not dating," Joe responded.

A wave of relief washed over Ed's face.

He moved one of his hands from mine and held onto the side of my face, rubbing my check gently with his thumb.

"Trust me. I know how beautiful you are. You get more beautiful by the second".

I couldn't help how much I started to blush. I could literally feel my cheeks turning red.

'I'm so sorry Sarah. Please can we talk about this in my car".

I looked to Michelle, and she gave a nod of approval.

Edmond stood up and stretched out his hand to me. This time I held onto it and we walked together hand in hand towards the exit. I could feel the eyes piercing through my body and the slight mummers within the crowd but I didn't care. I was finally getting my Ed back.

Edmond

Although I felt elated, I couldn't help but think about how disappointed my parents would be when they found out what I did. I held onto Sarah's hand a little tighter and smiled at her. I knew it was all going to be worth it.

As we stepped outside Hutchinson's house, Sarah looked even more beautiful in the moonlight. I could see the full beauty of her dress.

"Wow you're still wearing the watch I gave you I see," I said as I lifted up her hand in the air.

"It goes with my outfit," Sarah responded cheekily.

We got into my car, and I started to drive. The car journey was silent and a little awkward. I didn't know where to start. I didn't want to say the wrong thing and potentially lose her.

"Evans and Linda intend to go after my family's business," I blurted out.

"I know."

"You do?"

"You should have trusted me. I can't be with you if you can't trust my ability to process important information."

Had I already said the wrong thing? For flips sake.

"I'm sorry. I was thinking too much. I overthought everything. I didn't know what to do. I had to do the right thing for my parents, but I don't really care anymore. I can't afford to be unhappy. I don't want to live with any regrets. What's the point of living if I can't be with the one that makes me happy?"

Tears started to form in my eyes. I quickly took out a hanky from my breast pocket and pressed it against my eyes.

"I want to take you home, Sarah. I want my parents to know that I've changed my mind."

"I don't know if this is a good idea. Maybe you need to think about this really well. I don't want to be the reason everything fell apart."

"No. You're the reason everything will come back together. I have to do this. I have to fight for us."

"How am I sure you won't run of steam in a week?"

"If that happens, don't give me another chance."

Silence prevailed in the car.

I took brief glances at Sarah's face whilst trying to remain focused on the road. She looked confused and broken. It hurt so much to see her like this, but I was willing to do whatever it took to make it right.

SARAH

I was filled with tension on the drive to Edmond's home. I kept turning towards him. It felt like I was caught up in a dream but being with Edmond always left me with this sort of feeling.

It was a slightly long journey and my insecurities came to the top of my mind, making the journey even longer.

Linda didn't look like something I could easily get rid of. She looked like she was going home to pick another weapon from her armory.

I knew she was capable of bringing another twist to our story, and I didn't even know whether I was in the right position to see her as a villain.

Perhaps I was the villain. I was taking the love that used to belong to her. I looked through the side of the window and wondered whether this was a battle I could survive.

I wanted to believe that Edmond's action would serve as an impetus for Linda to finally give up on the feelings that kept her attached to him, but I knew I would be deluding myself if I held this notion.

It seemed I was going to have to hope that Edmond would choose me every time no matter the situation. Only, I knew, based on previous intimations, that I couldn't really count on it. Perhaps he would always love me, but I wasn't sure he would always defend what we have. To be fair, he was making a sacrifice that wouldn't be easy to make. But how long would he continue to trade off other things for his love for me?

"Do you think we can be together forever?" I asked.

"Yes," he replied, keeping his eyes on the road.

"I have doubts, Ed."

"I don't blame you at all. I've been so unstable."

"You would defend our love forever?"

"I'm willing to leave everything behind if my family decide to stand against us. I have my own company. I'm doing great for myself."

Edmond took a glimpse at me and turned back to the road.

"I have been thinking about this for some time. I know I'm ready. And I'm sorry for not being completely sincere with you."

His words were comforting, but it wasn't enough to quell the doubtful voices in my head.

Edmond weaved his hand around my wrist and led me into his father's mansion.

Mr. Barker was on the phone in the living room. Mrs. Barker was beside her, seemingly worried.

Edmond stopped at the door and watched them carefully. Mr. Barker kept nodding and kept his face down.

"I'll have to speak with him first," Barker said, and hung up. He looked towards the door and froze.

Edmond started forward, resolute and serious.

"I just received a call from Evans. What happened at the party?" Mr. Barker asked, seriously.

"Mom, Dad, I'm sorry but I don't love Linda anymore. I want to be with Sarah."

I had never felt so nervous in all my life. My palms started to sweat ferociously in Ed's but I tried as hard as possible to keep a smile on my face.

Mr. and Mrs. Barker exchanged glances and turned towards us. Mrs. Barker leaned closer and grabbed her husband's hand.

"Welcome Sarah. You've met us at a difficult time. Please sit down," Barker said, softly.

"Thank you," I said, and sat down on a couch. Edmond sat beside me and dropped his hand on my shoulder.

His parents sat together on a couch that overlooked us.

"I don't want you to talk about that business anymore, Father. I cannot be sold to please Linda and her family."

Mr. Barker stood up and walked away from the living room. He drifted to a miniature bar at the side and returned with a bottle of whiskey and a glass.

He served the glass, took a gulp, and cleared his throat.

"I have a bit of good news for you," Barker said.

"Good news?" Edmond asked.

"Yeah. Michelle Hutchinson contacted me last week on behalf of her father."

"Why?" Edmond asked.

"They told me they had secured funding to buy out the other shareholders."

"But Evans had an agreement in place."

"Yeah but the legal fee for breaking that agreement is one point five million dollars. Hutchinson was willing to outbid Evans and pay the legal fee."

"How did that go?"

"The deal was secured on Friday."

"What?"

"I was going to tell you tonight. I'm sorry Son. I know how miserable you've been lately and I have been feeling so guilty knowing that I put you in this position, but I didn't know how to fix it."

Edmond stood from the couch and charged towards his father. He embraced him, tightly, and kissed him several times.

Despite his mom keeping a calm posture, I could see how much Edmond's reaction warmed her heart. She used the back of her sleeve to wipe away the tears in the corners of her eyes.

"This is really good news," Edmond said ecstatically.

"it is and we'll be spreading their shares across your company. Hutchinson is willing to reduce his stake in the family's business for fifteen percent share in your own company. I'll leave that to you."

Edmond turned towards me. He had a big smile on his face. I wasn't sure I had seen him so happy. He came to me, dropped down on his knees, and placed his head on my thighs.

"Nothing is going to stop us anymore," he whispered, raising his face up. Edmond placed his hands on my cheeks. "Today is one of the happiest days of my life."

I didn't know whether I was numb or inundated by the information I was exposed to, but I managed a smile.

Mr. Barker walked towards us with his wife.

"Edmond really loves you. He's been miserable ever since. I know because I was in his shoes once," Mr. Barker said softly.

Edmond looked confused.

"In my shoes?" Edmond asked, standing upright.

"It's a long story Son but love came through for us. I hope this is beginning of something beautiful for you two," Mrs. Barker said.

Edmond took me to his duplex home. In the living room, he stopped beside the table and turned to face me.

He placed his hands on my cheeks and drew closer to me.

"Why does this feel like a dream?" I asked.

"Because the universe wants us to be together," he responded laughing.

"It's a bit scary don't you think? Everything is literally just falling into place."

"Isn't that what we've always wanted?"

"Yeah, but I didn't think it'll happen like this."

"Love has given us a bridge, Honey. We should walk through it."

"I am scared, but I really want to be with you," I responded.

"It's okay to be scared, but we are going to deal with any issue together," he said, and kissed me.

The touch of his lips sent serious vibrations through my body, and when he sucked my bottom lip, my whole body responded to it.

His hands squeezed my buttocks, furling up my dress. It felt like I was going to explode from the kisses of his lips.

I reeled backward and dropped down in a couch. He dropped down with me and continued from where he left off. His hands smooched my thighs and his tongue found its way into my mouth.

I was breathing heavily, but I was willing to choke from his intense kisses.

He hitched my dress up to my stomach, taking charge of my thighs. I felt his hand on my crotch and felt flushes run up my spine.

He looked into my eyes.

"I want you so much. Life is not beautiful without you," he said, breathing heavily.

"I just want this feeling to continue forever," I responded.

He smiled and started kissing me again. This time, his hand went for the zip at the side of my dress. He zipped it down and dragged it from my body.

I returned the favor. I ripped off his shirt, before getting on my knees to unzip his pants. I dragged them off his body, along with his boxers.

I stayed on my knees as I watched his penis rise in front of me. I held it tightly in my hand, sliding my hand up and down.

I looked up into Edmond's eyes as I licked the top of his penis before putting the whole thing in my mouth. Edmond grabbed hold of my hair as my mouth bounced up and down on his erection. He let out intense moans with every move I made. I could feel his legs shaking against my body.

As I came to an end, Edmond continued to kiss me intensely before he lifted me up and carried me up the stairs to his room.

He carried me to the bed and dropped me down.

Edmond laid on top of me. For a second, he just looked at me and smiled.

"I love you, Sarah Barry."

"I love you more, Edmond Barker."

Printed in Great Britain
by Amazon

27019140R00079